THE PHANTOM QUEEN

MIKI WARD

Blurb

My name is Rigan. It means queen. There's more... men call me Morrigan––great queen. Some fear me, some love me. I like it that way. Living in my forest alone with my crows and my sexy raven is my life. The days go by in quiet beauty, sometimes I'm not so quiet. You know that I'm a shifter. But, I have more than one form and they are all deadly. Some are lovely some are not. Especially now that someone has killed my love. I will get my revenge. This is a story of gods and men, a story from my life and what made me who I am today––the Phantom Queen.

Cover design provided by Nichole Witholder-Rainy Day Graphic
Design/Editing by Erica Collins
Formatted by Vicki M Duran

Contents

The Phantom Queen
    Note from the Authors
    To our Readers...

NOTE FROM THE AUTHOR

This is a work of fiction. Names, characters, businesses, places, events, locales, and incidents are either the products of the author's imaginations or used in a fictitious manner. Any resemblance to actual persons, living or dead, or actual events is purely used as fiction. I have tried to recreate events, locales, and conversations from memories of them. In order to maintain their anonymity in some instance I have change the names of individuals and places, I may have changed some identifying characteristics and details such as physical properties, occupations, and places of residence.

TO MY READERS...

Thank you for purchasing this book and reading it! Please don't be afraid to leave a review if you like it. I hope you as the readers enjoy this book as much as I enjoyed writing it. Be warned: It is recommended for ages 18+. This book contains graphic sex scenes, violence, paranormal events, and language.

Sincerely Yours,
Miki Ward

I dedicate this book to the ones I love across the veil.

-Miki

\

1

THE GODDESS

I'm the goddess of this dark woodland. If you call me, I'll come to you no matter where you are. Men sometimes call me the Morrigan. I have many names. My mother, Ernmas, calls me Rigan which means queen, others add the Mor or great to flatter me. Either that, or because of the terror they feel in my presence. I prefer the name my mom gave me. I'm not great, I'm just me. Maybe, I'm feared because I'm a shifter. I'm careful to shift alone, to spare them. The lengths I go to, ha-ha, they fear me. I can't help but love that. I stay here in the forest because I cherish it and need to be alone to gather the paths of men. The more I observe the world breathe, the more I perceive what will transpire. I let a lot of it happen but divert many of things I see. My goal is to protect the people of this realm. That protection extends to humans, plants, and animals alike. I stop...

I hear and sense druids in my forest. They seek me. I wait. The fall air is crisp, and their footsteps light though they're making the dry leaves crackle in their wake. The moon is full and shines with a smile. A smile I perceive in my heart. I raise a fog so the holy men can't find me until I'm ready. Mist curls off the ground and winds around the trees in a thick curtain keeping us hidden.

I sit patiently waiting in this tree with my crows and ravens. My lover, Bran is beside me in his raven form keeping me company. He's a son of the sea god Lyr. We're listening, gathering information while the druids search. It's not that they are stupid, far from it. Druids are the most intelligent of my people on the isle. I have set them over the tribes so the clans will flourish. Many of these geniuses are scientists, astrologers, architects, and gifted leaders. My folk aren't hungry or sick because of the mages care for them.

These wise men need to speak to me, their goddess. They believe they need information, so they can do a better job of protecting their charges. But, I'm the one in control and will tell them what will hurry them along a path I choose for their lives. Sometimes I prefer the hard road of war to get a much-desired outcome. My little ones are hard-headed and resist, not knowing what's best––what will lead to peace. The most appealing road won't make them stronger or strive for excellence. I need them strong in mind, body, soul, and spirit so they can become the legends of tomorrow... to not die out and stagnate.

Sitting on my perch, I hear one of my druids called Gearoid say, "Cian, do you feel the Phantom Queen in the forest?"

"Yes, I do, it's eerie and lovely at the same time, isn't it?" answers Cian.

Gearoid continues, "Please, get the others and settle them here under the trees. This open place is good. No fire.

She'll come to us when she's ready. Always give her the respect of making the first move, and she'll surprise you."

Cian gathers the group of druid seers and talks to them quietly. They form a circle around him and listen to their instructor. He's teaching them to sense my presence. I adore that... and that they're waiting.

My attention is taken by a wave in time. I still and watch it... a battle between the tribesmen soon––that has to be stopped. I see intruders that will invade quickly after if it's allowed to happen. If I let the people kill themselves off, we won't have enough soldiers to fight them and keep the land. All paths show this battle if I stop it there will be a more significant price to pay and the interlopers will absorb my people into the new group. A foreign race who knows nothing of respect for the gods and goddesses of our island. I understand I'll need the help of Dagda, the king of the Tuatha de Danann. He's the druid and chieftain of my tribe.

I mind speak to my lover, *"Bran, I need to speak with, Dagda, will you send a soldier to petition the king for me?"* Not waiting for his reply, I continue, *"I better make my presence known to the wizards now. Cover me."*

He turns and sends Finn to Tír na nÓg, the part of the Otherworld where the deities live. I realize I'm staring, even in raven form Bran is gorgeous. He's fierce and confident as he flies to the crows getting them ready with a sharp alarm caw and breaking the silence.

I call back my fog. It dissipates into the aether. I lift off my branch and fly, my love, and the crows at once surrounding me in a swirl of black feathers. Caws, rusty with disuse, announce my arrival to the wizards below as I fly toward the group. With a flurry of ebony plumes, I step out of the birds as a woman. Bran stays in his raven form and sits on my shoulder. The druids suck in their breath at my little show and bow before me. They think I'm gorgeous and desire me. That makes me happy. Now, that's sexy... to arouse these handsome druids. They are magnificent, a few of them are students who abstain from sex to learn control. They are on fire with need, but they control themselves admirably. Their lust is a spark to my own.

"Bran, you will have to calm the flame in me later," I laugh.

The raven shifter's small lift at the corner of his beak and the spark in his eyes makes my want blaze and core tingle. He growls, *"That will be my pleasure, beloved."*

I motion the prostrate petitioners to rise. "Gearoid, thank you for the respect you've shown my companions and me. You and your students are welcome in the Forest of Rigan. I have information for you but tell me first, why you are here?"

"We are here, Queen Rigan to beg for help and advice. The tribes are unhappy and jealous of the beauty of the men and women in surrounding tribes. They plan to raid and kidnap those they crave for themselves. You remember the daughters and sons of Criostoir? They are known for their good looks and clever ideas, and they are the intended targets."

I walk around a log on the ground between us looking down. I raise my gaze to him, take his hand in mine, and croon, "My druids, I have a lot to tell you. Make us a place to relax while we talk, and I'll tell you about the waves of destiny we control."

Without question, each druid flows around the small opening in the forest under the trees and creates a comfortable place to sit and talk.

2

THE DRUIDS

*T*he young druid takes my hand, Cian leads me over to a log he's found in the field, he cleans it and puts a red pillow top over it. There's a small piece of twig sewn to the side. I know it's one of his treasures. It tells me something about him. He motions for me to be seated. The druid leader says, "My queen, please sit here." Oh, I admire his deep lilting voice.

When I'm sitting, he asks, "Is it enough? Are you comfortable? Should I find something better?"

"Don't question it Cian. It's fine. When you show this level of care, even if it were the dirt where you seat me, it's enough," I reply.

He's a big muscular man. When he touches me he's gentle as if I'm a tiny rabbit, he's found in the field. When he moves, my view is of the others in the group. They're standing in a circle with my log seat somewhat raised from their own. I nod for them to sit, they obey without a word or sigh. Several are sitting the ground on small mats, but most are on logs, a few sharing. I know them. They're mine.

My voice low to draw them in I start, "To stop the battles between the tribes, let them gather. You stay hidden until the last minute, then walk into the gap between the two armies and hold up your arms. Call me, and I'll be there to settle the people. The masses fear me as the Morrigan crow but the battlefield they think they'll die if they see me. This will cause them to return to their homes without lifting a hand to one another. I've seen it and declare it will be so. The trouble you're experiencing with the tribes happens in good times—it'll soon end. War is coming to our island. Fomorians are coming; they are dangerous ice people, monsters, and a few are giants. Have your village warriors train for the fight. Show the women with children and elders how to evade an enemy. We need to build up our people to survive as a nation. Now, reach out your hands."

Obedient to a fault they extend their palms in my direction. A globe of light floats from me to them. I put one in each hand and say, "Keep this safe its power that makes others listen to you. Beware. The minute you're unfaithful with your words or deeds, I'll take it from you. Now, fold your fingers over the magic and absorb it into souls."

I delight in the sensual moans as they do what I asked. A few put their closed fists against their breasts. Most are in a daze. I wait to say anything, letting them soak in the sensation of fire in their innermost selves. I spot a wood nymph poking her head out of her tree. The little redhead smiles at me, giggles, and disappears. One of the women here speaks getting my attention.

Sorcha is a small druid with long auburn locks. She has her hair pinned back from her face and is the first to speak. Her strength is amazing. She asks, "Goddess I have a gift. A song for you. Is it all right if I sing it for you?"

"Ahh, little one you don't have to repay my favor. I'll be happy to accept the song though, Sorcha." What a woman she is... giving me a present... it flatters me.

The young girl pulls out a cruit, a small oblong string instrument with a wooden neck, and rests it on her knee. She plucks the six strings in a haunting melody and sings with a rich alto voice.

I sing of Rigan of the tribes and the island. Her
beauty captures us. Her love snares. What
will happen if she doesn't care?

She guides us with gentle and sure hands,
protecting our lives and lands. Pray, we never
discover what will happen if she doesn't care?

The mists bring the crow, raven, war, and the
wolf kin.
Hope you never see them, or it will be your end.
If you happen to see our goddess, the queen a dark
beauty, she will make you thrive.
The atmosphere around her gives life.
Treat her well or suffer for your mistake. You will
not live tosee the dark queen's hate.

I sing of Rigan of the tribes and the island. Her
beauty captures us. Her love snares. What
will happen if she doesn't care?

EVEN THE TREES sigh with the beauty of the melody as it fades. This forest is alive and knows what's happening despite what people think. When I morph into a tree, I can even sense they're a family with a deep attachment for each other.

Gearoid gives me a tankard of warm honey mead. It warms my hands, and I'm glad for it and put them both around the vessel. "Tell me how your family is Gearoid. Tell me the funny stories... and of the children," I ask.

He begins, his rich voice rumbling in time, he tells me of his offspring who fight with each other but then can't sleep away from each other. I laugh at the image as the pictures flicker through my mind. Now, my druids each have tales to share of their families and villages. When everyone calms, I bring fog and cover the clearing. They close their eyes in slumber and fall into a dream state where I remind them how to stop the battles between the tribes. When they are under, I share a thought with Bran, *"I'm changing, let's go find a place to work off my... desire."*

"I have just the place, follow me, my love."

Bran takes me deep into the woods until we reach a waterfall that's surrounded by the forest. There's a pool of fresh blue water at the base of the falling water. My sexy man doesn't stop the way I want so I can immerse myself in the landscape but flies straight into the downpour and into a cave. I spy mistletoe; I love mistletoe. It's beautiful in here. He shifts in a split second, and so do I. Glancing around I recognize he's been planning this rendezvous. There's a pile of bedding and pillows away from the water's spray. He sets light from globes aglow with a wave of his hand, at the same time he lights a small fire for warmth.

"That's the extent of my magic, beautiful. Is it enough?

Whatever you want I'll make it happen." His countenance melts my heart.

It feels like the wind on my skin when he reaches for me, making me shiver. I stiffen, something dark is coming, but before he can notice my reaction, I reach for him. His deep eyes bore into my own with a look of pure hunger. I try to live in the moment. I intend to make this moment unforgettable, stepping into him I surprise him by trying to throw him to the ground. Not surprised even a little by my move, warrior that he is, he catches me around the waist and throws me over his shoulder with a twist he lays me on the bedding with a sureness only great strength can accomplish.

Fine if I can't dazzle him that way... I make my clothes fade away and disappear. My nipples pebble, my core is wet, I'm ready for more and so is he. My naked body sparking his passion. He laughs, it sounds like music. Watching him remove his clothes, I squirm. He's a dream which makes my heart beat throb and my blood rush to my nether parts. A big man, and all mine, with dark hair and eyes, muscles sculpt his entire body, not the long and willowy but full round masses. I greedily take in his erect cock, licking my lips as he bends and leans in to kiss me. He whispers his love into my ear kissing and nuzzling before moving to my neck. It sends shivers of desire over my skin. His hand runs from my shoulder to my tight nipples. His kisses move to those pinnacles of nerves, and I reach for his erection.

He softly pushes my fingers back, "Let me have my way first Rigan, then you can show me your appreciation." He teases with a crooked grin.

I nod and suck in my breath as he touches my wet folds with one hand and brushes down my clit with the other bringing me to the brink of orgasm. I ride the edge of the thrill. When he moves over my body and finally flicks his tongue over my throbbing center, I groan his name. My fingers rake into his glorious black curls. He continues, and my legs shake with the sensations I moan and shatter. That's enough waiting, and he penetrates my still pulsing core. I meet him thrust for thrust speeding up when he does, he keeps on until exploding inside me. His face is screwed in passion and when opens his eyes... the look of love fills my heart to bursting.

The night moves on with passion, and we finally fall exhausted into each other's arms and sleep.

3

MY ENGAGEMENT

I stretch as I wake then turn to Bran, unable to hold back I smooth a hand over his hard chest then push a dark lock away from his face. What a wonderful thing to be loved by this man. He opens his eyes and looks into mine, pulling me close. I can hear his heartbeat.

Breaking the moment, I ask, "Are you as hungry as I am?"

He laughs and his chest bounces. "Probably not my love. No one can eat as much as you when you're hungry."

I back away just far enough to reach behind me to grab a pillow and hit him with it. He pushes me back and tickles me until I beg forgiveness before he relents and kisses me softly.

He says, "Rigan there are fish in the pond and I have bread and cheese here with a couple of apples. Is that enough or shall we hunt?"

"What if we have the bread, cheese, and fruit then, go hunt?"

"That is fine with me, even more fun."

We both get up and straighten up the bedding. I hadn't

paid attention the night before but there's a shelf with food and books on one of the cave walls. In front of it is a small table made of oak. I dress and look over the books and glimpse a small wooden box. Wondering what it is I pick it up and show Bran what I have. He tilts his head in a shy way I'm not used to seeing and says, "Open it, it's a gift I made for you, not much but made with love."

I open the box slowly and inside is a torque of braided gold wire with a carved crow and raven. The wings of the birds are open and facing each other in a diamond shape, the detail is astonishing. I suck in my breath. Excited! Does this mean what I think it means? My heart is beating out of my chest. I wait for a second then say, "Bran, what... umm... I stammer.

"My love, you are my life. Will you do me the honor of becoming my bride?" He takes the box and sets it on the shelf then takes the necklace and waits for my answer.

Tears of joy run down my face. I nod my head to him with gleaming eyes and squeak out a yes. Sex between gods is one thing and common. Real relationships and marriage are a whole different ball of wax. Marriage to us is a forever bond where we can even share talents if we choose. He turns me gently and lifts my hair. I reach for it and hold it for him as he twists the treasure around my neck. I drop my hair and lunge at him putting my arm around his neck and laughing as he swings me around in a circle.

"You have made me the happiest god in all the worlds, Rigan."

"And you have made me the happiest goddess!"

I can't quit touching the golden jewel around my neck as we prepare our food then sit and eat breakfast. When we're finished I shift into my wolf and he into his raven. We spend the rest of the morning hunting. It isn't long when my wolf self scents a deer in the area and follows the odor. I don't wait when I find my prey. Pouncing on it I savagely tear it' s throat out. It's a quick and generous kill and fills my belly. Beside me my raven god takes what he needs, and we leave the rest to other animals that have gathered who are waiting for a turn at the fresh meat. The crows descend upon the prize. There will be nothing left but bones very soon.

Earlier I had told Bran about the vision of the enemy who is coming to our island before I told the druids. Now, while we walk in the forest we talk more on the subject. planning what to do. We settle on our actions, he and some of the other shifters will go recognizance the beaches and set guards. While he's doing that I'm going to the village of Torn where I have business with one of my people.

My handsome man kisses me softly as we prepare to leave. I lean into his broad chest and smell his salty scent, breathing it in deeply. Shifting to his raven self he is ready to leave so I say my goodbyes and watch as he flies away.

One of my lovely ladies is going to have her child tonight and this child is going to be a catalyst for change. The sweet babe's mother is named Eva and she doesn't know the baby is coming yet, I'll wake her tonight and help with the labor. The older children will sleep right through if we're lucky. For some reason, I don't see the destiny of my village tonight the way I usually do. I'll have to wait and see what's in store later after the baby gets here safely. Maybe there's just too much happiness to see in one night. I hurry though the forest almost skipping I'm so happy. I better cut that out, someone might see!

The wind is picking up and blows back my long black locks. To keep it from tangling in the bushes, I change into my wolf. There are miles to walk to get to the village. When I morph the feeling is most carnal, my senses expand. Enjoying the sensation, I breathe deeply this is one reasons I like to live alone in the forest. Being on my own gives me more freedom, it would scare some the humans if they saw what I just did. At least the ones who don't know my wolf or my crow shape. Some would be excited and others greedy who would want the power. Shifting in private keeps the peace. My people can come to me when they need something for healing, otherwise I'll get a vision or warning and go to them to avert the danger. Sometimes, if I'm late, I can heal them or guide them to the otherworld. When this happens, they might be added to my spirit army or helping support the army of my darklings. There are those who I send to rest, but many help for a while before they rest.

The smell of cooking attracts my attention and I spot the villages round huts. Getting to the village early is a plus, I'm going to need some rest. I'll be awake most of the night to be sure. I'll stay here at the edge of the woods and relax. I stretch and lengthen my body into a yew tree, the people won't notice me. Changing, I find the other yew, hawthorn, and oak trees around me are happy that I'm with them. They know I need rest and sing me a melody on the breeze to ease me into a nap.

4

NEW LIFE

The trees around me creak and groan. I draw back my shape and re-join the world in my human form. A flock of my crows stays with me as I stroll into the village of Torn where the baby is about to be born. The moon shines bright, and I can see my path easily. Even though I see well enough in the dark, the glow of the moon lights my path. Before I enter the round wattle and mud house, I send one of my birds to get Eimer, the village druid. She'll help me and be a witness to the birth. The rest of my throng of preening black friends perch on the thatch roof. I go straight in without announcing myself it's my prerogative, everybody is asleep anyhow.

"It's time... wake up Eva. The babe is ready to come and meet her mother. Wake up little one, I'm here to help."

I wave my hand over her and blow softly over my hands sending a slight breeze over her. She moans and stirs waking from a restless sleep. A sharp contraction starts, and she sits first then stands. Standing she stops for a breath and holds her protruding stomach. A groan escapes her then seeing me she holds out a hand for me to take.

"It's time for the babe, goddess, queen of birth. Thank you for coming to make sure my child's birth is safe. I was afraid you might not be able to be here," she says grating her teeth as another pain takes her, and I know this will be quick.

"I've been waiting for this birth, helping my people is what I do, and I love doing it. Especially, ushering in a new life, anyway I want to protect you in case there's trouble."

Eva smiles, and I walk with her. It's our practice to walk and stay standing as long as possible, but her pains are coming quickly and force us to stop every few steps. I snake an arm around her for assistance. Eimer is here, comes up to us, and puts her arm around on the other side of the wobbling woman. The druid touches my arm, starts, then gives me a searching look to be sure it's all right with me. I nod to assure her she's doing the right thing.

"Eimer, where is this birth taking place? The last time you had a separate hut you were using. I like the idea––much cleaner. It's time, we only have minutes, are you ready?" I ask.

She understands what I'm asking, "We have clean water that's been boiled and filtered through sand, blankets, and enough cloths to wash the baby and Eva. Great queen, I've been ready all week. I believed the birth would happen at the full moon, but I've been wrong before. Please, come this way, it's the same hut as the last birth. I'm starting to call it the healer's hut because it's easier to help there. Like you said, it's clean, and my supplies are ready."

"I like it too because this way I won't wake the kids or Liran. Thank you, Eimer, oh-oh," Eva adds. She shuffles along and drags out another groan before we arrive in the druid's healing cottage. The uncomfortable mother lies on the bed, so we can check her progress. It's only minutes. She's been through this several times and understands more than we do that it's time.

The healer gets everything ready even drops a gold coin into the water she has set out to bathe the child. We check that all the door locks are open, and I say, "Any nasty little fairies who would try steal the child will be scared away the minute they notice me." Turning I put a ward on the village, just to be safe. This ensures no one can exchange the baby for a weak changeling. The faeries steal them to pay off debts to the god of hell.

"It's time for me to push, Great Queen," Eva manages. I stand before her, and the child is delivered into my hands in a few contractions. The caul is around her head. I lift her, showing Eimer and the young mother, discarding the caul at the same time. This little girl is crying in seconds. I hand her to Eimer, so she can clean her up and wrap her in a new blanket.

Eva says dreamily, "I knew it, I knew this child would have luck, but now she's blessed us all by being born that way." Weak and tired from the labor she flops back on the bed letting us take care of her precious infant.

Eimer is singing a song of protection over the baby. I notice that there is too much blood and investigate. Yes, the newly delivered mother is bleeding too much. I put my hand on her and feel her life diminishing. I stall and take a few seconds to see into the future. It's necessary for her to raise her children for a little longer, so instead of helping her to find the way to the Otherworld for rest, I heal her torn body. Even though this young mother has many sons, she'll have one more. But this little girl is the only daughter she'll have.

I glance up, Eimer is holding the baby close and watching me wondering what I saw.

I say, "It's better now. She'll survive this time healer."

As a learned one of my druids, I'm sure Eimer understands what I'm saying. She'll keep it to herself as I expect and teach. She lays the little bundle in the recovered patient's arms and laughs when the newborn is rooting for a nipple as soon as she feels her mother's breast. Now, that *is* good luck. I sing a song over all my girls in the hut for their protection and their health. I want them healthy and happy, and sense they know this, they care for me too. At the same time as I bend to kiss the new mother and child, I motion for Eimer to follow me outside. She's right behind me.

I say, "Thank you, daughter, you were a great help. I'll announce the birth of the child to the father. Stay with Eva and tell her he'll be here soon to announce his daughter to the village. It's wise to use lavender oil on her stretch marks but add a touch to her tea for healing. Not much though, use a nettle tea every day for a while."

The sun is just coming over the horizon, and we stand together to greet the new day. Afterward, I leave, I get to tell Liran he has a daughter! When I find him, he's bubbling over with happiness, "Thank you for all you do for us here in Torn. Especially, helping bring my daughter into the world. I have a gift for you great goddess, Rigan." He hands me a bowl of fresh hazelnuts and an apple, he looks so pleased with himself it makes me smile.

I accept the gift to honor him in return. He gives me the present with a good heart and makes me happy. The truth is, I'm famished and will eat it as soon as possible.

"Goodbye, my son, protect your family... even from within," I warn. Moving off and giving a wave I hurry into the trees. Once hidden I change into my wolf and head to the edge of the forest. This is far enough, I switch into an elder tree to give a gift of my own to commemorate the birth in the village. I grow a lot of purple berries and listen to the children of Torn later in the day as they giggle and gather them. With joy in my heart I fall into a trance and cherish the time to reflect. Sometimes to move forward it's necessary for me to stand still and watch... just living in the present.

5

A CHANGE

I'm jerked out of my reverie with a vision. Fuck! It's a terrible scene... Bran is hurt. I've got to hurry! I alert the crows around me, and I'm changing. They rise from my branches, change, and we fly as fast as possible to my beloved raven. Time flashes by as I race to him.

I see him, now. He's lying on a ledge above the crashing sea. He's still living but mortally wounded. When my feet touch the ground, I hurry to where he is lying on the rocks in his raven form. Someone shot him out of the air with an arrow, and he is dying. His blood is bright in the surrounding grayness.

Looking ahead, I take a few seconds to glimpse the future. It's sure on every possible path that he'll be terribly crippled, shamed by his state, and will be in agony until he finally passes through the veil. There is no choice! I'm forced to usher him into the kingdom of the dead. My heart! How can I survive without you? I waver and don't want to carry out the inevitable. Can do this for him? I love him too much to watch him live in agony for my selfishness. I reach for him with loving tenderness. I pick up his bloody body gathering him close to my breast. The banshee's screams pierce through the gathering mist. Three times I hear her screech. The crows caw above us circling the cliffs where we huddle.

"Bran, it isn't a good future I see for you, my love. Do you wish to come with me to the Otherworld? I'll make you a general in my army of the dead?" I cry. I force my words as I try to get them out for him. He's able to morph into his man form and settles into me. I sit for a time rocking him unable to move.

"I'm not afraid, my love. I trust you to know what's best, go ahead. I'll follow you," his voice weak.

I sit back on the cold rocky ledge, my spirit takes hold of him, and we travel between the realms until I get to a place of calmness in one of the heavens. I place him on an altar and sing over him as I dance around the plain. His corporal form crumbles and disappears from the platform. He's gone… I collapse to the ground my heart torn with the loss.

I scream into the aether, "Fucking Hell! Rejoice, you have him, and I don't. Why? You could have warned me? Why? I could have protected him!" I hurt terribly, my rage relieves the pain some. Even knowing I'll see him again in the army of the dead, it's not enough––everything is changed.

I stop yelling to the sky to sob into the dirt I can feel Danu is present, her earthy scent surrounds me. Even though I can't see the mother goddess, she calms me with a soft, cool breeze and then I hear her airy voice.

"Rigan, it's a horrible deep hurt to lose one you love, I'm sorry you are traveling this road. Come, child."

I get up and walk forward, and she is reaching for me and wraps me in loving arms rocking me like a baby. I cry, the tears spill down my face unrestrained until I fall asleep in the arms of the great Earth mother.

When I wake I'm curled in a hollow depression in the earth, trees hide me away. It smells like sweet apples in this place. I'm finished with tears, and my anger is rising. It's clear to me that I've got a mission. First, I'll find the person who took Bran's life and made me bring him to the Otherworld. I'll take them down! They will rue the day they killed him. My face will be the last thing they see. I want them to know who is ending their miserable existence. My anger is a tangible thing, and I refuse to control it. The fog of my emotion is thick over this realm.

I say through clenched teeth, "Thank you Danu for being with me and keeping me safe while I cried. I won't forget. I understand you don't show yourself often, but please come visit me when you have the time or the inclination. I'll honor your ways on the Earth and teach my druids to show the tribes your ways. Be at peace honored mother."

Trying to leave this heaven is hard, and I pause... waiting... I don't want to leave the last place I saw Bran. No, I have to leave. I need to find a murderer and kill them. I backtrack, needing to go to the ledge and gather clues. There might be a trail that will help me find the killer.

Upon my arrival, my best friend is here, his long white locks flying in the wind. He reaches for me as soon I set my foot on the ground. His big arms surround me with love, and he sings me a few lines of a bawdy tune of the sea that makes me relax and smile. Manannan Mac Lir is one of the gods of the sea. He's broad and brawny, his sword Fragrach hangs at his side. Good. I might need to borrow that! His horse Enbarr stands behind him a way off, munching on the grass and pays us no attention. I glimpse Mac Lir's cloak hanging over the saddle. Satisfied I'm loved I step away from his hug.

"Thank you, Mac." I've called him that since childhood, "for being here for me. Is it possible you have information about what happened to Bran? Something I can use to find his murderer?" I ask.

"Yes, but I'm here mostly to comfort you. Lovely lady, you know I would have ferried Bran to the Otherworld, but I understand you needing to do it yourself. Can I do anything to help, love?"

"No, nothing can make this better. I want to find the one who did it and flay them alive! Will you come with me to my home in the forest and tell me what you know?"

"That's a wonderful idea, little bird. Let me tell Enbarr, I'll return later, then we can be on our way."

I walk with him to the ebony horse and watch him smooth the animal's long mane talking to him and telling him he'll return later.

I step closer and say, "I'm sorry I haven't greeted you yet, Enbarr I wasn't thinking." I flatten my hand on the horse smoothing the side of his powerful neck, then conjure an apple and hold it out to him. With big sloppy bites, he eats it, then licks my hand when he's finished making me giggle. The black steed looks into my eyes, and I would swear he is smiling at me.

Mac pats his horse on the cheek and says, "You big flirt she's not interested in you that way. I'll be back tonight or tomorrow, if I'm not, come and retrieve my drunk ass from the village closest to the Forest of Rigan."

With that, I take Mac's hand in mine, and we shape-shift into wolves and run to the forest. I run as fast as I ever have, and my big friend spends no effort in keeping up with me.

He's fun and knocks me with his shoulder a few times play-fully. I think the next time he does it I'll surprise him. It's not long, and we enter my forest, and he pushes me nearly over. I let him, and with a yelp I circle him and hit him in the butt. It has absolutely no effect other than to make him chuckle at the absurdity that I thought he might fall. It makes me laugh though and speed up until we get to my little cottage in the trees. I sense no danger or strangeness, so I morph into my woman self while Mac shifts to a man form.

"That was fun, and I needed it, Mac." *How strange is it I can go from crying, to angry, to laughing? I must be going a little crazy. Who could blame me?* "Would you like tea?" I ask.

He nods as I move the kettle to the fireplace and light a flame with a wave and a growl. "That would be nice, do you have honey too?"

"Yes, you silly god. Do you need to be sweeter, aren't sweet enough already? I can name several women who think you are."

"I need as much as I can get," He says in a saucy tone. "I could name a few who have wanted you the same way, Rigan. Namely, your dream lover with the pale blue eyes you always see in visions."

"Shut-up, you dog," I punch his brawny arm and laugh. "That's just a little girl's vision... things change in those." I have shared my whole life with Mac and have probably shared too many of my dreams.

We settle into cushions I'd put on the floor in front of the fire. I pour our tea and hand him his. His big hand makes the large cup look like it was made for a child. Now, time for business, he relays the circumstances of the previous day. I feel myself needing the information and my heart freezing over at the same time.

6

CRUEL INTENT

*S*itting forward and listening to my best friend Mac as he relates the circumstances of Bran's murder I calm and burn with a desire to maim. I memorize every detail. I'll need them later.

Mac relates, "Yesterday, started out as a perfect day at the beach, sweet bird, then stuff happened quickly." I remain quiet as he continues, his serious voice thick with sorrow.

Bran is Mac's half-brother, and they loved to spend time together. Once long-ago Bran made up a poem for the sea god. One with which a man who was close enough to hear it sang it all over the island. It's known in the annals and libraries of rich men everywhere.

Mac says, "You and I know a group of Fomorians live here on the island and have for many years. Last week, another bunch rowed to the beach below the cliffs where Bran was shot. I thought they came to visit their fellow countrymen who live here and didn't think it was necessary to alert the gods who might not know about them. It's true, they went to talk to the Fomorians who live here but were rejected by them. They left their kin then and returned to the cliff-side. I couldn't hear what they argued about. I was too far away, but my men in the area told me the tale, and I understand it was an angry encounter. When they reached the rocks below the cliff, I could see them from the water. I stood and watched them on the waves with my cloak of invisibility for cover. That's when Bran flew over, and one of the scum took aim and shot him before I could move. I prayed for Danu to send you a vision and raced to capture the murderers. There are only three of them. I imprisoned them in a cave. I contained them in a cell with little effort on my part. I asked the sea creature Dord to guard them. He is watching them now. Funny thing was, I told them I was exacting revenge for my brother whose life they took with an arrow. They had the gall to deny what I'd seen with my own eyes. When I returned to the rocky cliff, you were ushering Bran to the Otherworld. I stayed in the area to be there when you returned."

"Why would they deny killing him? That makes no sense. Where did you put the vile killer's, Mac? I want to question them," I say holding my temper by a thread.

"I left them in a cave under the cliff where Bran fell, before the water's edge. More Fomorians are coming on the sea. I've seen the ships. They will land on the island soon if I let them," Mac says.

"I really need to question them. Will you show me where they are, Mac?"

"This minute? I promise, they can't get out of their prison. Don't you need food first?

"No, are you hungry? I have fruit and bread here," I offer. My stomach turns as I tell him this, I remember the last meal my raven and I shared. I set out the food for him, and he eats ravenously. It won't be enough for him, but it'll take the edge off of his hunger.

I remember something, "Mac you said others are coming by boat. I saw a vision of the ice monsters and giants coming to our island a few days ago. Finn has gone to ask Dagda for an audience and his help. Will you help me construct a plan, so we can conquer this foe as they land... before they can do any more damage? It's a sure thing they don't come in peace from my visions. I intend to exact revenge for Bran's death on this race of murderers. Be warned, I won't stop until they're all destroyed." I feel my ire rising. I'm sure, not angry at the sea god for not killing the murderous villains. That will be my pleasure. The one who shot the arrow deserves death. My blood is thirsty for revenge, and I'll take it as soon as possible. There's a knock at the door, so I go to answer it with a look at Mac he raises his cloak and is invisible to the visitor.

Finn, one of my warrior crows, is standing on the other side of the doorway when I open it and looks famished. "Come in Finn, I have news you need, have you spoken to Dagda? Will he grant me an audience?"

"I have, great queen, and he'll be here in the morning as dawn breaks. He said to meet him in the clearing of the pool at dawn."

Come in, sit, I have something I need to tell you. I know you loved Bran... He was scouting the cliffs outside the forest and was shot down by a Fomorian arrow and killed. I transported him myself to my favorite heaven in the Otherworld. I feel rage building again as the look on Finn's face falls.

"What has happened, my queen? Do you have information on the killers? I'll hunt down the murderers and bring them to you for revenge immediately." Finn says fisting his hands and getting ready to leave.

I reach for his shoulder and touch him to calm him. "I have more, noble crow. The raven god was searching, as you know, for information about invaders to our country. I've had a vision, and he was seeking a way to thwart them when he was struck down. Also, Manannan Mac Lir was watching and imprisoned Bran's killers when I was ushering him through the veil. We're going to question them now. I'll spell them because they deny the murder. Will you come with us?" I ask.

Then he notices Mac standing beside me and nods his assent. Without further talking, we change into crows and fly. With Mac in the lead as a cloud, we make our way to the cave prison.

7

REVENGE

*M*ac leads us to the small cave under the rocky ledge where Bran met his end. I stiffen when I spot his dark blood staining the rocks as we pass over. My anger is sparked to a flame. The prisoners won't survive this day. I'll make that happen, by my own hand. Mac isn't one to kill, even though I have seen him angry, he holds his lightning for other purposes. I'm good with that... this is for me.

The cold spray from the sea is raging on the rocks in front of the opening as we enter. The foreigners aren't fooled by our shapes and watch as we shift into human form. I decide that they don't get to see the pretty goddess, Rigan. They get a scary old toothless hag. They get the Mor-Rigan. Spotting me, they back away from the bars of the constructed cage Mac has them in. I try not to gloat. The sea god bows to me and leaves me to my business not interfering, but I know if I need him he'll be here for me.

Finn unsheathes a knife and comes at them and threatens, "Vile human scum. Why did you kill the raven god? Who is your king?"

"Please," they beg, "we didn't kill anyone. We're here to meet with our families who never returned to us and bring them home. Once we talked to them, they told us to leave. They love the land here and don't want to return to the frozen lands of our ancestors in the north. We left them after they all but threw us out of their villages."

My voice is acid as I accuse the killers of the lies. "You tell us one small truth and then lie. What are you withholding?" I demand.

"Nothing, oh great Mor-Rigan..." I grab him around his scrawny throat and squeeze cutting off his words.

"Tell the truth, and I'll let you die quickly with little pain. I promise."

The man next to him asks, "Great queen, promise me this deal and I'll tell you."

Nodding at him I say, "Continue."

Continue is what he does with a shaky voice and body. He says, "We have been sent to scout this island, so our Lord and king can take power over it easily. We went to our people here, but to warn them to fight with us or die. They say they will fight with the inhabitants here rather than with us. So when we made the beach, in anger Gruen fired into the air and killed the raven without even aiming. I'm sorry that it happened, Great Queen, we can't bring him back." He shakes his head looking at the ground still trembling. When he looks back up at me, I can tell he's accepted his doom. "Our kin will be here in two days if they have had luck on the sea and will battle for your land. They are celebrated warriors and admired for their skills at war. And we have a strong god-king who intends to take this land."

I reach out a clawed finger and pierce his head digging deep I kill him quickly as promised with a smile on my wrinkled face. I pucker my wrinkled lips and blow a curse on him to serve the army of the dead until I release him. I turn and see that Mac is there to usher him to the Otherworld. I let him and proceed to the other prisoners. They won't have it so easy. My hatred is flaming hot.

I send Finn to watch the entrance of the cave while I work. Mac will have others in a while to take to the otherworld, but I'm going to make their torture last as long as I can. I laugh as I start. My revenge begins here.

I don't know how long I've been torturing the assholes, but I've had enough. I'm tired and numb. Exhausted, I've finished my work, and the murderers lie damned at my feet in a pile of gore. I let the men die slowly and leave them lying cursed and bloody on the cave floor. Blood smeared, I change into my beauty and nod to Finn as I leap into the sea to remove the repellant filth of my enemies. My anger is deep. Even so, I'm not happy, but I do feel like I've done right for my love. Walking to the beach, I clear my head. I stop and stand on the edge of the water and shout to the air above me. "Bran you are avenged!"

Mac has brought a storm for me to revel in and I watch as lightning lights up the dark sky. Getting hold of myself, I gather my crows and fly to the forest to rest before I go to meet the king of the Tuatha de. I have a deal to make with him so he'll help me defeat the foe that's coming to our shores in just two days.

Hopefully, I can offer magic he'll accept, or maybe... payment of future magic helping him. Perhaps it will take the beauty, I'll try that first. I think he's known to love a good romp. I'll tie the god of life to me, the queen of death, that way if he's willing. Then we'll conquer our enemies. He'll get what he craves, fun, the life of the land, the people who live here alive and well. And I'll get what I also want––more blood of my enemy. The army of the Tuatha De Danann is a must. I can't defeat the advancing army without them, or I'll be ushering most of my island's tribes to the Otherworld. Yes, I'm sure he'll take me up on my proposition. With that in mind, I fall to sleep and dream of the coming battle.

8

THE DAGDA

*L*ater, when I wake, I run as my wolf to the pool to wash as the sun rises. I change to human shape stand in the little waterfall and never enter the small cave I now is behind the water. It hurts me to think of it and tears run down my cheeks. I wash away some of my pain and try to think of happy times spent with Bran.

Shaking off my sorrow I continue to clean my body. I plan to be as enticing as possible to the Fae King. I'd met him briefly in the past, but he has many consorts. How interesting can a woman be to a man who has so many women? The sun is rising, and the warmth is nice on my body but unnecessary. I'm letting the cold fuel my plan. My nipples are as hard as stone, and my flesh has goosebumps as I raise my hands to lose my hair. I'm taking out the last of nine braids I'd put into it, and my dark strands wash down my back in a wet shining wave. I feel the presence of the Dagda and let him gawk as much as he wants before I turn and look through my lashes at him. He's not fooled and knows I've set this trap for him. He climbs off of his horse and walks across the rocky ground toward me then stops, his lustful bulge evident.

Without words, I see he's decided to let me have my way for a while. He removes his clothes and stands in all his glory for me to look him over. I do and take my time. Dagda is beautiful. His face is one to inspire bards with his long wavy hair and beard and spikes my desire for him. There is no other hair on his masculine figure. I love that he is sporting a pair of magnificent horns for me, similar to the antlers of a large buck. His body is muscular, and his Adonis vee to his nether region is pronounced. My body is ready and wants him to fill me. I squirm and rub my legs together and walk toward him. He is making the air warmer just with his presence.

"Mor-Rigan, have you asked for me here for a tryst? I would have come to you anywhere to spend time with you. I had the idea that you wanted something else from the message you sent. I'm not rejecting you, don't think that, my beauty. I'm ready now, but I want to be sure this is what you want. I'll give you what you ask without it."

I take a second to decide reaching to smooth my fingers over my necklace. No, I see we are partners on the waves of time, we enjoy each other. I don't believe this relationship is something hurting Bran in any way. Bran and I can't have that kind of relationship. This isn't that kind of love this is want and need. Yes, I do want this, and Dagda will be a living asset.

"First, I want your body to please mine then we can talk of the other reasons I needed you before," I answer.

Without questions, he walks to me, and his big muscular body leans into mine, and he takes my face in both hands and tells me, "With pleasure, my beauty." He crushes his lips to mine and devours any words I might have said. I forget speech and rub my body against his.

He's excited and as erect as a young man with his first woman in his arms. My hands smooth his chest and moving upward I thread my hands into his hair. Need pushes me, I arch into him and groan out loud. He bends into me with little bites and nibbles on my neck making my core throb with need. Moving to my breast he sucks on them. I shudder. I reach between our bodies to play with his smooth hardness. His hands move to explore more of my body, and he presses me closer to him. He's amazingly strong. My legs raise in response to his urging and circle his waist. Our excitement builds. He walks closer to the rocky wall beside the fall and holds me pinned there. I guide him inside me, he enters stretching and filling me to the brink. I scream into the morning air. I almost come with him entering me. In minutes he's pounding an intense orgasm out of me. His timing is perfect, and he grunts at the same moment he comes.

The Tuatha king moves me over and gently sets my feet upon the ground then he scoops me back up and walks to the forest where with a nod and a flourish of his great horns makes us a house in the trees. He carries me inside and lays with me on a bed of fine linen. Relaxing he wraps his strong arms around me falls asleep. He smells spicy, and I melt into his warmth and sleep.

When he wakes, he brushes the hair from my face. I open my eyes to his sky-blue depths.

He says, "Rigan, that was worth all my time, I wouldn't change what happened between. I have a feeling... it might have a little to do with grief for you though. I share your grief. Is it possible you care for me... just a little?"

"Dagda, yes my grief for my love Bran, is intense, and I won't forget him or his love. I do care for you. I didn't know I would, but I trust you. Is it enough to start with? Even if we're very different, I want you in my life. I think maybe life and death may have more in common than I'd known. Is it odd that sex helped with my grief?"

"I'm happy with that then. About the grief, if I have helped ease a small bit that makes me glad too. Did you know your lover was one of my brothers, the youngest? I'll miss him too."

"No, I didn't know? I'm so sorry for your loss too, Dagda. I don't know what to say. So Manannan Mac Lir is also your brother. How did I miss this? He has been my best friend for my entire life."

"Thank you, little crow. Mac has told me about you frequently, but we are gods over different areas and many years separate us. Now, tell me little death crow why am I here?"

There is a lot to tell so I start, "I've seen a tremendous Fomorian army invading our coasts, killing many and bringing ruin to our island. These are the people who murdered Bran. I'm asking for your help and that of your army to help defeat this enemy."

The great god of life gets up from the bed and looks for a kettle. He lights a fire in a stone fireplace. I can't help myself and rake his nude body with my eyes. His muscles bunch as he moves around making us tea. When he conjured this house, he filled it full of things we would need. After making our tea he sets two cups on a table close to the fire. He sits his large frame in a chair and motions for me to take the one opposite from him.

I get up and dress in a robe from the end of the bed. The

silky material soft on my skin and swishes as I walk over to sit with Dagda.

He says, "Tell me more Rigan, my prize, so I have details for my commanders, so I'm not leading them into this battle blind."

I proceed to tell him everything I know about the advancing army, including that Mac will help having seen Bran shot from the air the day before. A lot has happened in such a short time. I brush my hands on the torque at my neck taking comfort in it.

Dagda leans forward and kneels in the floor in front of me placing his hands on mine with his finger on my chin. He says, "For you, I'll do this," then he kisses me softly.

I'm so happy I push into him and deepen the kiss and wrap my arms around him. I can't help the tears sliding down my face. He understands and kisses them away.

After we enjoy each other's bodies, we spend the rest of the day planning our war strategy and sharing our resources. However much I'd like it, he can't stay and must return to Faery to get his army ready. I need to deal with the tribes and their foolish battle. Then must get the people the information that the real enemy will come to our island in another day.

The king of the Tuatha leaves me with a kiss to my forehead and makes me smile before he's gone in the breath of an instant. I spend the rest of the night in the tree house. I like it here and plan to make it my home.

9

THE MORRIGAN

I hear my druids calling me. It's happening now! I gather my crows and fly to the battlefield where the tribes are fighting over their petty argument. I spot Gearoid, Cian, and also little Sorcha. They all have their hands raised just as I told them and are calling me. They're in an empty row of land separating two groups of armed men who are ready to fight.

I swoop in and circle with my crows and keep flying over the battlefield. We are cawing noisily. The soldiers see us. Some drop their weapons in fear and prostrate themselves. To see me means death and they're trying to get me to let them live.

I say, *"Finn, I'm changing so I can speak with these idiot men. Let's make it a grand entry!"* It's a spectacle as we flutter and swoop close to the Earth with the surrounding crows. I change into my warrior maiden guise. Both armies groan with fear. I flourish my blade and back them away from my druids.

In a loud voice, I shout at the idiots with disdain. "Who are the leaders of these armies? Come forward if you want to live."

Two men from each group come forward. Their heads up they look me in the eyes. I have to give it to them for their bravery. One kneels in front of me and says, "I'm your servant, Great Queen. My name is Tomas. If it's your will we die today, let it be in your service."

The other warrior taking the queue from Tomas also kneels and says, "Yes, let it be so, my queen. My name is Zander, and I'll do whatever you command. We are yours."

I answer, "Well, that makes this much easier Tomas and Zander, my servants. We have death to bring today, but not to each other. Do you have a place to talk and plan? We have only hours then we need to meet the real enemy at the sea."

Zander gets to his feet and motions for his men to part, showing me into a small tent littered with maps of the area and full of extra weapons.

Many in each of the armies shrink back as I pass, fear written on their faces. I like it. I want them to listen, and fear is a great weapon.

Entering the tent first Zander says, "Please sit." He makes a point of brushing off a chair for me. I take it, and he points to another for Tomas.

I start, "There's an army of Fomorian warriors on its way to our coast. We must defend ourselves, or they will decimate us, and the people of the isle will disappear. The enemy will land close to nightfall. Manannan Mac Lir said he'll send a storm, so the invaders will be at a disadvantage. The sea god plans to hit them as soon as they land. None of us wish for them to hurt or destroy anyone or thing on our island. We will have the help of the Tuatha de Danann for this battle. With them, the battle should be easy to win, but we need to start now to get to the coast. What do you say to a real fight for something more than lust for another's family? Maybe you will earn each other's respect and make honorable contracts for the marriages you seek." I notice that both of the leaders are turning green from my news.

Zander turns his face severe and stony. He says, "My men and I are at your service Mor-Rigan. Will you lead the men, or shall we meet you at the coast?"

"I'll be with you as you start, then I'll guarantee the enemy hasn't landed sooner than we expected. I also need to talk to my sisters and ask them to help," I answer.

Tomas reaches for the hand of his opponent in conciliation. He says, "We find ourselves on the same side of this battle Zander Mac Dole, will you vouch that my tribesmen will be safe from yours during this fight? I promise in return that none of my men will harm yours until we resolve this battle. At that time, I hope won't have anymore arguments and you will allow my kinsmen to ask for the hand of your daughters in marriage."

Tomas answers, "I agree to your terms and will ask my tribesmen to reconsider marriage options with your people when the time comes, and we're successful."

I add, "You two also need to understand, this battle is with giants and monsters that come from the Viking seas. The Fomorians will use their looks as an advantage to overcome us. Prepare your men, so they aren't surprised. We don't want them dying because they are frozen in fear. I trust they will fight with all they have when the time comes."

They nod that they grasp my words and hold the tent

flap open for me as I leave. I stand in front of the tent while they go to their respective armies. The warriors need to see I'm with them for the fight. As their leaders meet them, they inform them about the circumstances that we will meet a terrible and very real enemy. The soldiers respond as the tough men they are. All are willing to meet the army of the Fomorians in the battle tonight with no reservations. In fact, some men say they are ready to leave this minute and don't want to keep their goddess waiting. That sends up a glad shout, and I smile. I'll get my revenge, and it will be sweet. I will watch my heroic people and hope they all make it home safe, but if they don't, I'll take them to the Otherworld in high fashion and make sure they are honored for their service.

The armies have become one army now and with me at its head. I shift into my crow and fly in front. My crow brothers and sisters fly with me. After several miles, I'm sure they can make the rest trip to the shore without me. I change my course and go to my sisters in Faery to speak to them and ask for their help.

I'M in luck when I reach Badb's home because Macha is with her. Both of them are like me. We're stronger together, and I love to fight with them against a common enemy. Badb is like me in that she's a war crow and vicious in battle. Macha is also similar to me in that she's a fantastic warrior, but she also loves to make a big deal of decapitated heads in a fight. She is good at it too, usually putting the worst warrior's heads on pikes to show off. I laugh at that every-time she does it. That's one reason she takes such glee in the process. A good laugh is priceless.

Badb croons, "What do we owe the pleasure sister? I haven't seen you for a while. Is everything in the human realm going all right? Are you, all right?"

"No, I've come for your help. I know you know what happened to Bran because I heard you scream the Bean Sidhe's call before he passed, so you know that I'm grieving for him," I answer. That was hard to say, I almost choked, but this isn't the time.

Macha wraps me up in a hug, she didn't miss my grief. Her hair touches my cheeks and smells like flowers. She says, "Let me make us some tea, and you can tell us all about it." She is such a mother.

I enter my sister's kitchen and tell them everything that's happened. Time in the Faery is different from the human world. One day here is the same as a thousand on Earth sometimes, anyway. I take my time, there's no need to hurry. In the end, they love a good war so my sister's begin to prepare themselves to fight with me. We decided to show ourselves as crones for the fearful impact on the enemy at the beginning of the battle then change if the fight dictates.

I take each of their hands and travel the aether to the mortal realm and the coast where we meet with Dagda. He has such a regal flair and has his tent set up with pennants blowing in the wind.

He greets us, "Hello, sisters of doom. You look wonderful. The enemy will cringe when they gaze on your visage." He takes my hand with a grin and a bow.

"I laugh and ask him what he knows of the enemy. "Are they close? Have you seen the army of our men?"

The Fomorians are close, and the people of the island

are here. I set them behind the hills and will call them with a horn blast or signal from my harp when the enemy lands. We will overwhelm them before they know what has hit them.

So... we settle in and wait for the invaders to show.

10

AT THE SHORE

We investigate to the shores of the beach where we intend to battle for a short time, so my sisters know where we'll start. Afterwards, we return to the tent of Dagda and await the blood fest.

Looking up, I see Mac walking toward the tent where we're discussing our strategy. He says tilting his head, "Dagda, Rigan, sisters, you can catch the first ships of the enemy now if you look into the sea."

I rise to follow him. The heat of battle is on me now that I observe the enemy is almost here. The others are at my back and watching the water churn. With a wave of his great hands Mac sighs and chants a phrase. A flash of lightning lights up the horizon and a storm begins. My friend's eyes are white with his creation and the uproar intensifies. A shiver goes down my hunched spine and my crows circle over the bay then search for cover. The rest of us wait for the ships and the occupants to land. There are more than I'd thought would come, at least a hundred boats of various sizes. My visions are too limited sometimes, it's never a sure thing exactly what will happen. I might know that most of the time what I'm shown. Most of the time, I understand what I see isn't the whole truth.

Dagda stands behind me with his hands on my shoulders, He kisses the top of my head and says, "I'll be with you, Rigan, fight well, my blood is yours. I'll protect the best I can. You know I have faith you. I understand you'll be tireless in your revenge and will leave it to you. Unless, I notice you need me, then I'm butting in."

With that he leaves and walks to the sandy beach to his army nodding for Mac to bring him the enemy. The great druid chieftain takes his harp with him and strums a haunting tune. It reverberates though out the army and the men are immediately itching for battle. It pounds and vibrates in my chest making my nerves jump. The melody of the Dagda is the best trumpet call and we are instantly ready to start. The chieftains of the islands tribes stream over the hills at the call.

The king of the Tuatha de Danann gives our army a short pep talk, "Today we'll be bringing Death, and she won't hold back. I won't either. I have your backs. Protect the one next to you, your families, and your land."

My breath hitches from his words. I could care for him deeply if I let myself. Later, I'll think on little more, right now I need to concentrate. I see... the battle won't be easy, and some marauders will get away and steal into our island. That's okay, I'll hunt them all down and kill them. My hands move upwards and I raise a fog so thick I can taste the sea.

I watch Mac as he increases the violence of the storm. His beautiful long white hair blows away from his chiseled jaw. He muscles are so tight I can see his pulse throb in his throat. We can perceive the ships tossing, but only a couple are breaking up from the pressure. One slams into the reef and shatters. Some men are swimming toward the beach, some load into small boats. Many sink into the white caped waves. I blink spying them. Yes, there are most defiantly monsters with them, but many of the soldiers appear like pale, large human men. Their hair is long and braided for battle. I can recognize small trinkets tied to some of their braids, no doubt from prior battles. I've heard they believe the prizes will give them strength. Some are from loved ones, I'm sure. I don't care. They will die today.

My sisters hold my hands and we walk toward the sandy beach where the interlopers are making it to shore. When they glimpse us old crones they startle. That's the effect we wanted. Zander and his men are killing them easily. My sisters and I shift and prepare to launch into the air to meet the monsters. More who see us stop and stare. The Tuatha De are on them in seconds and they are past into the afterlife with no fanfare. Mac is delivering the entire Fomorian army to us swiftly on crashing waves in a stormy field. Having done his part with the storm, he now ushers the dead to the Otherworld. The rest of us keep him busy killing as fast as the enemy lands. There are so many... we have to be diligent and keep moving.

There's a monster coming straight toward me. Oh, I'm ready for this beast. He's a giant with only one eye, right in the middle of his brow. Where we have a space, he's got only one big eye. He isn't a fachan that's for sure; he has two arms and not just one coming from his chest. His pointed teeth don't fit into his mouth and are crooked and protruding. The colossus's movement is stealthy regardless of its size. I can tell he sees me as prey. I morph my talons into a hand with long claws. I smile and fly straight to him digging into his single eye. It's warm and sticky. I curl my digits and pull. His one eye pops out of the socket easier than I thought. I toss it on the ground with a gravelly noise that is actually a laugh only my crow guise can make—so evil sounding. The big cyclops is enraged now and swipes a big hand through the air hoping to kill or maim me. I'm too fast. I might look old like a hag sometimes, but I'm a goddess, and my crow body is able to avoid the flailing member.

My sisters are here now and on him, tearing at his body, coming off with large bloody chunks. My crows know he's prey and cover his body ripping and clawing bits out of his hide. He throws himself to the ground trying to dislodge his tormentors. It doesn't help. It makes it easier for them to tear at him. He is gone in minutes. I've already moved on not taking the time to relish the scene I morph into human form and fight on.

The smaller members of the enemy are a hardy bunch but kill just as easy. The Bean Sidhe/Badb cries without taking a break. Mac is finding that he must take several souls at once to the Otherworld. I glance around to find Dagda, he's an amazing warrior. He's using his cub, lorg mór, and claiming the lives of nine enemies at once. With his club he can kill or revive depending on the end of the club he is using and at this time he's killing.

The enemy is using archers. They are of little value. The Tuatha De can defuse our bodies when we see them coming, they travel though without harm. We can't fight that way though so don't keep ourselves in the transparent state. The humans are superb with their shields and clubs. Some have been hit. I bend and rip an arrow out of a warrior then blow air across my hand on the soldier at my feet to heal him. Some won't live today but our losses will be light. The man at my feet rises and nods his thanks, his back is to mine in an instant as we are mobbed by a group of the enemy scum. I can't help but grin as I tell the soldier to spin with me as I blow death on the ones who are close enough to feel the magic poison I have in my hand. They are falling all around us howling in pain. I shout my glee in victory. The field is a bloody disaster, and the enemy is retreating. I notice some are running into the forest and some over the hills. We will dispatch them as we find them. I won't allow them to live on my island. But I'm feeling better that we've killed so many of the ilk who took Bran. I change to my wolf and howl to the sky then lope over to Dagda.

Many times, during this battle I've watched as Dagda takes charge. He calls a rest and sets up guards around our camp before he sends soldiers to spy on the enemy with orders to report every hour.

Macha is running around collecting heads. The laughter bubbles up and I shift into my hag form. Laughing is so much better in this shape and I can't help but screech in delight. My sister decapitates a body then grabs his spear and plants the head with a sick splotch on the pole. She isn't stopping at one and makes a fence line on the battle-field with the heads of our enemy. She's winding down from her own rage. I stop watching and walk to the area of our tents.

When I reach our camp, I spot as Dagda fills his cauldron. It's one he calls coire ansic, the cauldron that never runs dry. He instructs his men to feed the army, and rest, this fight will start again in the morning. The scouting party he had sent out will guarantee we know what the invaders are doing. I notice he has his harp and is playing it... it heals the wounded. We're in a good location and will be able to hold the marauders. If this war takes too long, we'll have to retreat to the hills and change our tactics. For right now it seems that we can win this fight. I fill a plate and sit at the fire with Dagda and Mac to eat.

My sisters join us at our fire with their plates full of food and drink close. They seem fine, I'm glad to see it. They fight well and I'm glad they're here. We are a good team.

"What do you think, Dagda? Is the fight over, or will there be another battle tomorrow?" I ask.

"Death crow, you tell me," he asks.

I take a look into the waves of time... I still and breathe deeply then answer him. "I see this battle will rage for three days and we will kill, have some killed, and yet win the victory. There will be more of the enemy to battle and kill along the way. There will be a trial for you, Dagda, and a trial for us all then another victory. It all seems so easy to say what I've seen but without living through it I can't explain it any better. You understand that I can see things, but a lot gets left out, right?"

"It's enough, love. Will you change for me I'm weary of the hag and want to see your beauty? There are enough ugly spirits floating around from the dead tonight," He begs.

I smile changing; I'd forgotten I had changed into the hag laughing at Macha. What he says is true Mac has let many the spirits roam tonight and will catch up tomorrow with help of the other Tuatha de who can deliver the dead to the afterlife. I change for Dagda then lean into him to cuddle and he lets me. I'm full and drowsy. He puts his harp down and wraps both arms around me and says, "Sleep while you have time. I'll wake you later."

11

VICTORY

*I*t's early morning before sunrise. Dagda wakes me with a pat on my arm. Not startled, I smile up at him. I like his smiling face peering into mine, and that he's considerate enough to wake me. I rise with no worry of showing my naked body to him and get a drink of the tea he's set out for me. He reaches for me, and we kiss the kind of kiss that's sweet and promises more later. I bat his hands away playfully. We have no time for more and have to get ready and prepare ourselves for the fight.

After we're dressed and standing together in front of his tent, he takes my hands in his large ones. "Rigan, keep yourself safe today. If you need help call for me. I'll do my best for you today."

"It will not be an easy day, handsome," I relate.

He nods, pats me on the ass, and turns to give orders to the Tuatha army.

Walking away from him to find my sisters and prepare for the rising of the sun, that is doubtless when the enemy will strike again. When I find my siblings, they are teasing each other and braiding each other's hair. Actually, Macha is braiding Badb's red locks and just finishing binding it with a gold ribbon. Macha motions with her chin for me to sit in front of her so she can braid my hair also. She takes her only minutes to make a long braid and tie it with a blood red ribbon.

"Thank you, Macha," I say tucking my braid into the back of my shirt. No need to make it easy for the enemy to catch me with it.

"You are welcome, little sister. What is our fighting strategy today? Shall Badb and I stay with the crows and fight flying while you are on the ground or will you join us in the sky?" she wonders.

We will fight this battle for three days. One is behind us. I don't want you hurt, will you mind if I'm with the ground soldiers as a wolf and you in the air to warn me if I miss someone sneaking up on me?"

Badb says, "I like that plan. Just keep yourself safe too sister. You wouldn't want to lose a chance to be with that gorgeous god you have been hanging on lately. Don't think we haven't noticed it's more than just sex."

I reach for her, and she avoids the little slap laughing at me as we hear the ringing noise of the harp make our battle call. Our attitudes adjust immediately, and we are war ready. My siblings morph and fly off into the cloud of crows over our heads. I lock eyes with Dagda as I morph into my wolf, so he'll recognize me during the battle. His grin as I change is delightfully devilish. Yes, I like him.

Screams sound in the morning air, and the battle's begun. My crows are making an incredible racket. The smell of blood is strong in my nose and makes me ravenous. I run to the front and start my own fight. Raging now, I'm berserk with anger. I remember what we are fighting for even in my wolf shape. It's secondary to the rage and want for blood. I won't allow the people of my island or my island to suffer because of these brutes or be destroyed because of the invader's greed and power-hungry small minds. Ripping and tearing at them I'm covered with blood and gore. The taste is in my mouth, I enjoy it. I catch an unusually large opponent coming for me, and rush forward to intercept his charge. He's a giant troll. Blue with a short crop of dark hair that is only fuzz on his head and ugly face. His muscles bulge as he runs, he's immune to the spears being thrown by the soldiers around me. I leap into the air snapping at his throat. I catch his jugular in one bite tearing his jugular to shreds. His blood is acid in my mouth, so I spit it out. Sure he won't last, I turn searching for another foe to kill. I hear my sisters warn me and twist around looking for the problem. I'm too late. The dying giant's foot stomps me in his last efforts before death. He catches me on my back legs, crushing them into the rocky ground. I yelp, the pain is massive, and I scream for help. I don't have to wait. My handsome savior, Dagda, is here and picks me up as I black out.

NOW AWAKE I'm disoriented with pain but watch as Macha takes my legs and sets them for healing.

I scream at her, "Ow! It hurts, Macha!"

"Yes, it does and will hurt more. Now shift sister I can do a better job if you are in human shape. And stay still, so this works, and you don't have a deformed leg or hip. On the count of three, I'm going to set the bones in place. Can you stand it, or do I need to find someone to hold you still?"

"I can do it… find someone who will help me, please."

I realize my handsome Tuatha king reach to hold my body down as I drift in and out of consciousness. Is he taking time from the battle to see to me or is it over for today? I have to be strong. I don't want him to think I'm weak, so I grit my teeth and find a point in the sky to concentrate on. Macha doesn't wait and pulls my bones into place. The pain is beyond what I can control without a scream, and I screech. My strong lover's concern is written all over his face. That is the last thing I see as I pass out from the pain. I stir and listen to harp music. My body is numbing, and the song relieves my pain. The thoughts that go through my mind make a small dent then I quit paying any attention and sleep again. No dreams or future events bother my unconscious mind, I'm left in peace to heal.

Opening my eyes in the dark, I register I'm in the King's tent and he's snoring at my side but only touching me with his hand at my arm. I test my legs, and they're fine. Stiff but fine. Thank the gods for fast healing and a king who has a healing harp and uses it for my benefit.

I raise up to look at him. I take my time inspecting his body, from head to toe. He is beautiful. Rolling onto my side, I curl into him. I have no idea how many times I have heard that killing incites lust. Maybe that's why I feel desire building, but I think it is part of who Dagda is. The lusty want is like a compulsion he sends out of his being, but I won't wake him. I know he needs rest. He's been fighting like all the soldiers not just sitting and watching. Afterward, I'm sure he walked the camp to cheer the Tuatha de and soldiers and then take his harp to the druid healers' tent to help the patients they can't. His cauldron is also feeding this vast army. Even a god needs rest. He's doing a lot, and I for one am grateful. I snuggle deeper into his large hard frame and fall back to sleep until he wakes me for another day of war. I smile in my sleep at the thought of our victory.

12

SUMMONING THEM

*A*nother day of battle and the killing field is full of the dead. We lost many lives today. I've got to be quick to notice when someone is hurt so Dagda can get to them with his harp. My crows are picking at the dead like fruit. The Fomorians thought they would ambush us in our sleep this morning, but the guards were frosty and on their toes. They sounded the alert with battle horns, and our army was ready in seconds. I morphed at the first horn blast and met my sisters in the sky. Humans from the tribes are the ones who won this situation for us with their iron banded clubs, spears, and strength. The whole day was filled with brutal combat, and we are doing our best to finish this war. The Fomorians are wearing down now that they have lost so many lives and retreated to their camp.

The fighting over for today I've got to clean the blood and guts off of my body. Everywhere I look the sea is bloody with bodies. I'll wait until later and wipe off what I can with my hands.

At the end of the day, the scouts and druids report to

Dagda who is sitting with me at the fire drinking a cup of honey mead.

"My king," Gearoid starts, "Our scouts that have are keeping an eye on the enemy's camp have returned with good news. We need to know what to do with it and prepare. The invaders have planned to flank us after sunrise. The scouts also overheard them saying that they will win the day and if not, they can make their ships and leave this horrid land and savage fighters. What are our orders?"

"I think a horseshoe formation around the camp protecting both flanks to surprise them. Also, we'll leave guards on our rear. Give the orders to the generals, druid. I'm making today a holiday and calling it Samhain let the dead roam today and every year from now on at this time we'll leave the doors open for the dead. Someone tell Mac he doesn't have to work so hard tonight. Now if you please, I want to spend a few moments alone with my lady," says Dagda.

LAYING in his arms an hour later I can't help but feel adored. This closeness is so essential, and I love his big body snuggling up to mine.

I say, "Dagda, I can summon my darkling army from the Otherworld. There is a chance that they can help finish this war. I can only summon them once a century though, so we need to be sure that this is the time."

He answers, "Tell me exactly what the army of the dead can do for us."

"They can hold weapons and kill when summoned. Many times, the fear they instill is enough to scatter an invading army. They are not flesh and can possess a person making them freeze in fright so that another can kill them without a fight. Bran is with them, and he won't let the enemy harm me," I say.

Dagda thinks for a little while then says "We had heavy losses today Rigan. Let's risk it and get this over with. If there is another war, we can figure out something else. I don't want to take a chance you will be hurt again. I'm not ready to lose you... I'm getting very attached to you, beautiful. The extra protection has decided for me. Call them."

"I need to go now and will have them here by sunrise. I'll meet you on the battlefield," I say as I dress, bending to kiss him lightly. "Be safe Dagda, I have an idea that you need to be careful as well."

"I'll do my best. Don't worry about me and hurry back."

I shift to my crow and fly into the aether to the army of the dead, my darklings. When I fly the temperature plummets. I shiver but travel on, it's always this way when the dead are close. I can't enter their domain, but I can stand at the arch and summon them to me. Flying in a circle in the damp dark I wait... deciding if this is right. Yes, I think it is if they don't come I envision many more deaths and losing this island.

I gather my courage and summon Bran with my heart in my throat. It's as if he's been waiting for my call and he flies to me. We circle and swoop with the joy of being together. Then we sit on a nearby rock where there are no living plants, and talk. We can't touch, but the feelings that are evoked just being together have us laughing and reminiscing. He changes, so I also shift. Then he reaches to touch my necklace. His hand passes through and into my chest with an icy cold caress. I shiver, and he pulls away. I can't stop him but try, and my hand goes through his arm. Sadness and loss pound at me. Now that the mood is serious and the joy of seeing each other is passed. I tell him about what's happened with the Fomorians and the battles then ask, "We need the army of the dead Bran will you come to our aid?"

He answers, "My love, you just have to ask. I'll do everything in my power this side of the grave. I'm more than pleased you came, so I could be with you and see your beauty. However, don't you agree that this is one time I should be there to exact my revenge on the people who stole my life? A life that held so much promise?"

I suck in my breath and agree, "You're right! What was I thinking?" I answer my own question, "I've been thinking of my own loss and revenge. This is for you." His declaration has made me even more resolved that my dark army should fight this battle.

Time in the Otherworld is very different, and when the dead are concerned, it's even more so. I hold up a finger to him which he understands from experience, I need to I look again into the paths of time. He waits while I watch. I look to be sure we aren't overcome in this war. I see that no time has passed there at the battlefront as yet. It relaxes me knowing that and relay what I've witnessed to Bran. We have time to spend with each other. We talk more and plan that I'll come to visit him more and he'll visit me on Samhain.

He says, "I'm always making sure that you're all right via a pool of still water, they show the dead the living. I can blow a little breeze over you to let you know I'm watching, but he it's light, and you might not even feel it."

"No Bran, my beloved raven I'll try to pay attention and smile when I feel a breeze. You can tease me if you see me and it was not you when I see you next. Now, will you tell my darklings that they get some freedom today?" I ask.

"Stay here and say the words. We will join you and ride the aether together," he says.

I sit on my cold rock as he leaves, feeling bereft. Standing to my feet so I don't make them wait. I begin. When I've said the sacred words for the summoning. They stand before me in a heartbeat. I have protected the words so that no one can abuse them. The charm will die with me. If I ever do. I'm not planning on it being soon. Even though they aren't flesh and blood, they are mine, and I'll protect them.

Bran is informing them about the battle. They are strategizing their plans for the enemy. They already know that they will be able to hold weapons and must take them when they are on the field of battle. I look into time and see that it's time for us to be going and motion to Bran. I shift at the same time as he and we lead this dead army to the field to slaughter a deserving enemy.

13

SOME ESCAPE

*W*hen we arrive on the bloody battlefield flying through the aether, I summon fog. It's streaming like a snake through the ranks. I motion to Dagda, and he comes while Bran shifts into a ghoul worth fearing. I say, "Dagda, I'm back and have Bran and the army of the dead with me."

The Fae king smiles and says, "I'm happy to see you, Bran. Brother, I'm sorry I wasn't there for you. Forgive me, please. I intend to get revenge for your early death. Thank you for answering our fair queen's call. I know you didn't have to, but you and this army are needed. Is there anything I can do for you and what do you and your army need from my troops and us?"

Bran answers, "Thank you, brother. Maybe, there's something we can talk about later. The army of the dead and I are glad to be free for a while. I'll enjoy vengeance on the nation who caused my death. We can kill with the weapons from the fallen on the field and will hold the enemy sill as your men cut them down. Unless, you have a specific need, we can fulfill... I do need to talk to you when this is over."

"If I notice something that will work during the fight I'll signal you. I agree with your plan. It's more than sufficient." Dagda says and asks, "My queen, will you let me have a word in private with my brother and your general as you prepare for war? I only need a few minutes?"

"Of course," I answer then glance at Bran, leaving to find my sisters. I know they'll talk about me and I'm also sure I don't want to be there when they do.

When I find my sisters, they're plotting. That in itself should worry who they might be against. However, I'm not worried, I'm usually the one who gets to enjoy the show.

I ask, "What are you two talking about? And can I help? If I know you, this will be amazing." I laugh at the look of innocence they are faking.

Badb screeches a cackle, "Our dear sister has a plan. She's summoned a large herd of wild ponies to scatter the enemy on the field of battle with a stampede." She's laughing so hard she can't finish, so Macha takes up the story.

She adds, "I want to ask them if I can give them the gift of speech for an hour or two. I want them to say, 'die varmint' before they stomp the enemy to death."

With that, I'm bent over, my sides splitting with laughter. I ask, "And you couldn't come up with anything scarier sister?"

She answers, "Shut up! Both of you." I recognize she isn't mad and is smiling about her little joke. We hear the harp twang to warn us the invaders are engaging. We shift with a thought and fly, swiftly so people won't die alone and hoping they don't die at all.

Both Bran and Dagda arrived with the crows and are in the middle of the action. They are doing as they planned, while Bran sinks into the enemy holding them in place, the king stabs his long sword into them. Bran picks up a sword from the fallen man and brings death on a phenomenal number. Dagda puts his own sword away in favor of his club, lorg mór, he swings deftly, and nine rival soldiers die. I have a sad thought... it would be nice if he could touch Bran with the other end of his club the one that brings the dead to life. There are consequences I don't wish on Bran or anyone, really. When the club is used, it can't give the body back to the owner, and they return as zombies and decay until their bodies are gone. This makes their souls roam, unhappy without a body they haunt the living trying to inhabit them. I don't wish him to become a fetch... no that's not for my beloved.

Everything seems to benefit us until I watch something rising from the water. I fly closer to investigate. Stopping in mid-flight is difficult, in a flurry of wings and feathers I turn and away. Circling from my position in the sky I gape at what looks like real ice giants slog toward the battle. They told me of the ice giants but never saw one until today. They rise out of the sea like glass. They were held in reserve until dire need. This is the do or die situation for the Fomorians so it's time they show up for one last attempt at a victory.

I caw loudly! Both Bran and Dagda hear my warning and look up to see the three huge ice giants coming their way. The monsters must be at least ten feet tall. I'm going over strategies in my head panicking a little. What will kill these crystal monsters? Dagda answers my questioning thoughts instantly when he throws lorg mór at the beasts. Well, it's worth I try. His gambit gives him the victory as the first one shatters with a loud crack and spray of icy powder. The club returns to his hand when he stretches his palm forward toward it. He overtakes the remaining creatures with gusto while I hold off as many as I can by flying into their horrid faces with my flock of black death crows. They bat into the air until Dagda can throw at another. It feels like the minutes take hours as the next ice beast is hit with the death end of the king's club and disintegrates. One more and these are destroyed. I stop my onslaught in the icy face and let it go forward a few steps to fight with Dagda and see Bran sink into the form. It stops and turns then runs straight toward a large pile of rocks. He exits right as the monster crashes into the stones and is pulverized.

Relieved I continue to watch from the sky and see that the army of the dead have taken over and are demolishing the invaders. That's when I notice Macha's horses. She wasn't kidding when she said she asked for a stampede and they are complying. What lives the ghosts and army haven't claimed the wild ponies do. I think I can hear one of them say something, but I don't think it's 'die varmint.' I smile at the thought. I'm also relieved that the victory is soon at hand. I land shifting into my woman self and stand with my darkling army as Dagda comes toward me. We all stand together and watch as our army finishes the few invaders left. My king takes my hand, and I let him but look toward Bran. He's watching and has his 'I understand face' on but also just a slightly cocky grin. We must make a beautiful picture standing over the seen watching over the end of the fray.

I glimpse a group of enemy combatants make their way

into my woods. Others are heading into the hills, and I watch as a few run back the direction of their camps. Mostly the invaders are killed the few that escape I'll hunt down and deliver death to unmercifully. That will be my life until they are removed from this plain. I won't let any of them live. They came and sought to kill, and they will be the ones killed to return their favor to our island.

Mac comes to stand with us and after a silent moment he says, "I'll take the dead to rest. Do you have any requests Dagda? Anyone you would like in your death army Rigan? Bran, do you?"

Dagda answers first, "No, brother. I have no instruction, this is where you excel. Thank you, Manannan Mac Lir. I know you dislike taking lives and didn't expect you in the killing, but the storms were an immense help. The ushering of the dead to the otherworld will let me concentrate on the living. I'll see you again soon." He gives his sibling a hug and as they part with a pat on the shoulder. I hadn't even known they were related to the Tuatha king until I met Dagda at the falls. We gods and goddesses were born far apart, and many times even siblings have only one parent they share. The shock I feel realizing how much they do resemble must show somehow because the men seem to feel it. I guess I have an attraction for gods in the same family, even if Mac is just a friend. I have always thought he was terribly handsome. *Argh, quit thinking that! What have I done? Is it bad? Will it hurt them?*

Mac nods at him then his gaze lands on me questioning.

I answer, "I didn't realize that you were all family, Mac, just you and Bran. I only figured it out when Dagda told me you are brothers. Other than coloring you do look alike." Passing off my sudden discovery I move on to what I need now that the battle is finished. "It's time for me to help with the healing of our people with Dagda but is it too much to ask if you'll work with me to raise a fog around the island and make it invisible to invaders for a time?"

"Looks like the trick is on you then, Rigan," He chuckles. "And not in the least, I would love to raise fog with you. You're my best friend and will be for as long as you want me."

I turn to the two others and say, "Bran, do you have to leave? Can you wait a while, so I can say goodbye?"

"Yes, my love I have until morning before the Otherworld calls the army back and we can't cross," he says.

"If either of you needs me, I'll be close and see you both tonight." I say as I take my best friend's hand and we walk toward the rocky plain away from the battlefield.

Mac and I stand silent together looking at the water hand in hand. I raise my free hand and bring a thick blanket of white fog over the island. Mac blends his magic with mine, and we weave a security of sorts over the island. When we finish, I lean into him, and he puts his strong arms around me. We have more work though and part. I kiss him on the cheek, "Mac, thank you for being here for me. I'll see you later. You know how to find me?"

"I do." he takes a stone from his pouch and shows it to me. When we were younger, I had given it to him, so he could find me, thinking he would love me like a man loves a woman. That's not what we have, what we have is love, just not that kind. When he rubs it, it's like he's touching me. "I always have it with me. I love you, Rigan. I'll be here for you when you call me."

"I love you too."

Smiling I shift into my wolf self, he watches me until I

lope away. There's a lot of work to do before I get to rest. I'll start with my sisters and healing the wounded. Then I'll walk the camp and thank the cheiftains Tomas and Zander. They need to know they're free to go home and resolve their plans for their villages. Then I'll spend time with Bran. I don't want him to leave, but it's necessary.

14

A SURPRISE

The battlefield is still gruesome but better than it was before the armies started the cleanup. My eyes search out and land on Dagda. He's busy strumming his harp healing the wounded. My darklings are gathering bodies and creating two separate funeral pyres. One for each army. That seems like a good idea, they are only bodies now, the enemy pile has no heads. I know the humans will take comfort that their dead are being respected though. The parts with no body are being added to the closest pyre. My sisters are walking up. Macha asks, "Sister, why so much fog?"

I answer, "I want to protect the island from more invaders for a while. This way the island will be harder to find by sea. I want to hunt down and kill all the Fomorian enemies who escaped the battles before any more land. Mac helped me with the magic it'll keep us invisible. It won't last but it will for long enough."

They both agree that's good. Badb says, "So, we

already killed all the enemy wounded for you. We're tired. Can we go home?"

"Yes, sisters, go get some rest. I love you both and can't thank you enough for your help." They hug me tight and disappear into the fog. I listen to the clop of hooves on the rocks and figure Macha shifted into a horse. Now, I wonder if any of the wild ponies are still here. I search the area and find none. I hope my sister remembered to thank them, they were a great help. Dagda has healed the last of the human wounded. They aren't staying in the area but dispersing like everyone else. Bran and the army of the dead are finished with the pyres.

He glides toward me and stops to say, "My love, we are finished with our work here. I want to release the ghosts, they need freedom before sunrise?"

I blink and say, "Yes, yes, of course, they must enjoy every minute while they can."

My love turns and gives the message to the army, and they all drift away. It's only Dagda, Bran, and I left on the field. When the king sees we are the only ones here, he comes to us and asks. "Shall we say a few words or just light the pyres, my queen?"

"A few words maybe, then light them and let's go home to the tree house, please."

His serious demeanor relaxes some, and he starts his deep sing-song timber. "All the dead we salute you as you travel to the Otherworld to find a way to your rest. You have taught us lessons that we accept. Now, be released from any ties to this plain." Finished he throws his hands out and two balls of flame travel toward each pyre. We stand together, hand in hand and watch as they burn. At least Bran's hand is sunk into mine while Dagda's holds mine. I don't know what possesses me when I start to sing, but I sing a song to remember these fallen. The wind carries the haunting chorus. I pick up Mac singing with me from far away as we've been known to do in the past. When I finish, the men on each side of me look at me in wonder.

The king of the Tuatha de says, "The magic of your song made me calm, Rigan. Let's go home."

I nod and shift into my wolf. He changes into a large beauty of a buck. The antlers on his head majestic. Bran nods and I run as fast as I can to the forest... to my new home. As quickly as I ran, Dagda is sitting relaxed at the fire in the tree house, as if he's been waiting for hours. I laugh when I spot him, and so does Bran. He greets us and waves a hand to the other chairs.

We sit, and he starts, "My beauty, Bran, and I have talked, and we have a proposition to put to you. If you will?"

"Okay... what do you want to ask me?"

"I want you and so does he," He points to Bran's specter, "we've agreed that he can enter my body and together we will make love to you. In the morning, you understand that he'll be forced to leave. The Otherworld will call him after sunrise. But, you'll at least have had some of him. If you don't want to accept our plan that's fine, we understand. As it is, I have no problem accepting him as a guest in my body for tonight. It won't be like only one of us can know what is happening. We've tested how it feels on the battlefield. We both have full awareness at all times concerning what my body is doing, and I'll give him control equally. As brothers, we understand each other and think it comes easy for us. I love him, and he loves me. We think it can work. What do you think?"

I have many feelings popping up at the same time. First

shock, then happiness, then, *can I really be this selfish. Yes, I can! I want them both! Even if it's just for one night. I'll always have Bran in my heart, but this will be something to remember when we miss each other.*

I take a breath when Bran says with disappointment in his voice, "Rigan, if you aren't comfortable with the..."

I butt in, "No, not another word. I want you and I want Dagda too. Please do this for me. Let's all work this out together. I want a bath first, there's a lot of the battles left on me. I need to wash it away. Did you make a bathtub in this tree, or do I need to go to the waterfall?"

Dagda answers, "No bathtub yet, but I can add one higher up, maybe. But... watching you bathe in the fall took my breath away the first day I saw you. I could warm the water for you if you give me the pleasure again."

"Only if you shower with me, handsome," I flirt.

Bran nods and sends a look to Dagda to confirm, "Are you ready, big brother?"

The Tuatha king nods and stiffens as Bran's spirit melts into his brother's body. I'm giddy at the thought of having both of them at the same time. One of them speaks, and I have no doubt it's my beloved. This might be easier than I was thinking... telling them apart that is.

Bran says, "Last one down has to bring the soap and towels." He immediately shifts into a raven and flies.

Now, that's interesting, he can change Dagda's body into his bird form. I shift and fly after them. Since I can't figure out how to win this one, I'll let them have the victory. I'm not wasting time though and get to the pool anticipating the fun. No one is here. What do they have planned is the question? I melt my bloody clothes off and enter the pool, and as promised it's magically warm. I need to clean off, I want this to be special without the battle gore. I enter the fall and start to rinse off when I feel Dagda's hard body. He leans against my back, and I shiver with anticipation. He maneuvers me out of the direct spray then reaches around me with soap in his hands. As he lathers me up with a smooth, gentle motion, I sink back into him with a groan.

"You can keep that up all night handsome," I say.

"I could, but I have a better plan," Dagda returns.

I step into the spray and rinse off, turn, and take the soap from him and return the favor. My god, he's beautiful. His chest flinches when I touch him. The ripple of muscle is irresistible, and I brush across him using both hands. I turn him to rinse his upper body, and he goes willingly while I finish his lathering his hard body. He groans when my hands minister to his throbbing cock. I won't wait, and neither can he. He rinses off quickly then picks me up gently with his big hands and carries me through the water to the cave where he has towels. I watch as he takes one and wraps me in it and dries his own body. I help a little... and take my own towel, if I bend at the waist and let my hair fall forward, I can jiggle my tits while I dry it. The trick is making it, so he can see. I catch him drawing in a deep breath and glance at him through my lashes. Well well, that worked fast, ha-ha.

One step and I'm against him grinding my wetness against his leg. He lets me for just a second before his mouth crashes down onto mine. I can't even think anymore, and I refuse to try. I like to let my body take over sometimes. My back arches as he lowers me onto the pallet waiting for us. He allows me to play with his hard dick and never makes me stop––his control is so good. He flips me on top straddling him, and I sense he's ready. I raise up on my feet and guide him into my body. The stretch is amazing and I squeal my delight. He laughs, but I can see the hunger on his face as our passion mounts. My legs are getting shaky, and I sink down onto my knees and hug his chest while he thrusts up and we move faster to our orgasms. I come, but he is right behind me and says, "Fuck Rigan! I'm coming! Argh, you make me crazy."

I keep moving to enjoy the sensitivity, and he puts his hands on my waist to stop me. Bran chuckles, "A man can only take so much, love. It tickles too much. Let us rest... there *will* be more."

I sigh and lean into him and fall fast asleep. No way was I meaning to sleep when there are so few minutes left to spend with my raven. He is playing with my hair and wakes me.

Rigan, talk to me before I go love, I want to plan your visits to the Otherworld. I can't stand being without you. At least, I'll have that to look forward and not stress too much. That is what we do for the short time we have left. All too soon it's time for the sun to rise and he separates from Dagda.

The king says, "Brother, I'll miss you, I promise to make time to visit you. Thank the army of the dead for the victory, please."

We walk outside together to greet the sun. At the first touch of the warm rays Bran blows me a kiss as tears fall quietly and run down my face as he fades from view.

15

BECOMING A GUEST

*D*agda gathers me to him with strong arms, and I can't help but sob. He understands more than any living soul how I feel, and I trust him. After a while, I calm, and we walk back into the little cave to talk. The reality is, we are together, no words need to be said. I'm not hungry, but when he hands me an apple, I take it and eat.

Breaking the silence, he says, "Rigan if you would like to live with me in Faery you're welcome at the palace. You can have your own place, and I'll make sure it fills your every need.

Well, that wasn't what I was thinking... at all. "I'll take you up on the offer. Are you sure it won't be a problem, Dagda? With the politics involved, I don't want to hurt your standing or the power of your word."

He bursts out with big barrel laughter, "Rigan, your presence will only add to my power. In fact, beautiful, it's my opinion you'll make it much easier on me to give orders that will be carried out without question. You understand the respect and the fear you inspire, don't you?"

"Not really, but I guess you are right. When would you like to leave? Oh, and I could move back and forth between realms without being held back, right? I have villages and druids to watch over. And... Dagda, I plan to kill the invaders, every last stinking one of them."

"Rigan, I won't hold you back. You can kill the Fomorian invaders but remember we possess members on the island who came from there who aren't the enemy, okay?"

"I'll weed them out, and I'm ready when you are, my liege." I make a point of teasing him. I'm sure he understands I recognize he's the king and I'll take some of his orders.

He shifts into a large horned buck, and I take my cue from him and shift into my wolf. We run with wild abandon in the forest until he comes to a rocky hill where he sniffs the air and investigates the area.

I change and fly into the air catching on that he is making sure no one will find the opening to Faery by seeing us enter. The only things I see are the animals of the Earth. I swoop down and shift at the same time as I touch the ground. I like some drama. My king does too, evidenced by his chuckle.

"I saw no humans at all. We're safe to enter," I say.

"Yes, you're right, beautiful. I can't perceive a human for miles. Let's go in, get something to eat, and rest."

I follow him in through the wall it's just an illusion, there's an overlapping stone and a crack large enough for us to get through but no wider. This will be a trial for me, being around crowds, especially the court. I don't want to be alone, yet so I'll get through.

EVERY CELL in my body is on full alert. I haven't been here for a long time. The last time being when Bran and I met. Now that's a stab to my heart. I suck in a breath of the cleanest air and smell the sweetest scents. Every flower and fruit you can imagine mingled together. You would think that it would be terrible or overwhelming, but it's beautiful and calming. The light is different here, the way it is in my forest and it feels like a caress.

I lean into Dagda trying to hide away. I'm not shy. I've been in my forest alone with only those I trust for so long that introvert would be the most helpful way to understand my character. Maybe my old crone side is taking over, ha-ha. I might let it happen. I'm yanked out of my reverie when a skinny blonde presses up to my king with all too much familiarity.

"Oh, Dagda, my king I have missed you terribly." She laments with an exaggerated droll tone that reminds me of the reason I left Faery. That was because of the pretentious fools who live here. I roll my eyes about to step forward a little and brush her hands away from what I'm claiming for now when a brittle old man does it first.

He reaches in smoothly hands his king a cup of something and says, "Your Majesty, I'm so glad to see you home. Please, if you will..." and he motions for us to follow leaving the woman gapping like a beached carp.

"My lady, I'm the king's steward my name is Tornitch. If you need anything while you're here just ask, and I'll be at your service. I'll assign a maid and hairdresser to you. If you aren't happy with the ones, I choose I can always find another. Don't be afraid to tell me you want a replacement."

He leads us into a beautiful room that looks like a combination of an office and sitting room but with a definite masculine quality. It smells heavenly like pine but with a touch of sandalwood. I sink into a red leather couch and put my feet up on a dark stool that's close.

"Here love," Dagda hands me his drink. It's warm and spicy. I love it and smile at him for the favor. "Good save, Tornitch. I don't want to expel the flirts from the palace but make a proclamation while my consort is here no one is to put their hands on me without her consent."

The old steward nods and smiles then fills another cup from a table against the wall that appears is explicitly used for drinks. After handing a sizeable golden goblet to his king he says, "Your Majesty, I'll make it known. And, my lady goddess Mor-Rigan how shall I inform them you are to be addressed?"

"Now that Bran is passed and a phantom I'm still his queen." With my finger on my chin, I look into Dagda's eyes to be sure I don't hurt him. If I do, I'll notice, and I can make it up to him later. Tornitch, have them call me Goddess Consort Mor-Rigan or Phantom Queen. I grin, how is that... too much?"

"No, Rigan it's good to make a point as soon as possible before the courts take matters into their own hands. They won't be able to be as degrading as they would with a name that comes with a warning connotation." Then he laughs the loud bellow I love to hear.

Tornitch agrees, "Yes, Your Highness, I agree this is a perfect name, and I will relish the looks when I make it known." He slaps his hand down on the table for emphasis, gathers the empty dishes, and leaves with a wink then scoots through the door.

Dagda sits beside me and scoots me close. "Let's sit here and rest for a little while, Rigan. Then we can get you situated. I have a room connected to mine. Is that all right with you? I'll give you as much privacy as you need, but if you don't want any, I'm good with that too. As an added benefit if you need to be talked into it, there's a swimming pool and bath big enough for a troop. Does it help, I know how you like the water and so do I? How does it sound?"

I touch his face with both hands, "My handsome king, I'd love the room connected to yours. Privacy is something I want, but I don't want to be alone all the time either. I know if I'm left alone I'll prefer seclusion only to withdraw from people totally. Does that make any sense?"

"Yes, it does love. I understand. Let's make a deal here and now to always be honest with each other. It would be kind of hard for me not to know you having shared Bran's memories." He says as he takes my hand in his large one.

"I'll make the deal with you, Dagda. Promise me you won't go back on it. I really need you even if we become only friends again or if we become more. Things might change given our long lives, but please, I'll accept it as long as we always tell each other the truth."

"I promise," as if it seals the proclamation in blood a bond of magic swirls through the air and tightens around our touching hands with a tingle then dissolves. He leans back into the arm of the couch and brings his legs up pulling me close. I snuggle up and drift off with him for a much-needed rest.

16

ALONE IN THE PALACE

I'm rousing and don't want to move from my warm slumber when there's a quiet knock at the door. Dagda must have been awake, he gently moves, and we get up together. I smooth my hair as he answers the door and lets Tornitch in.

"My King," he bows slightly in my direction, "Your Highness. We have your room prepared. I prepared the room attached to yours, Your Majesty. If that isn't acceptable, I can change to another? But if it is, would you like to freshen up for dinner? I'm afraid that the crowds are gathering and would like to see you since your absence. It would be the perfect time to impress on them the importance of our guest."

"No, you read our minds. I wholly agree what do you think my little Phantom Queen?"

"I love the idea, you handsome horned god!" We laugh as we follow hand in hand to the rooms. I ignore the glances at our hands in the halls by several busybodies and overhear a snippet of a comment. Someone says, "Can you believe she has the gall to be with our king wearing the raven's work?" She is speaking about my gold torque.

I stiffen, and Dagda tightens his grip on my hand, pulls me to him. He gives me a positively hot display of public affection I'm sure will have the old hags gossiping for hours. I'm forgetting my name when Tornitch clears his throat. We glance over at him, and the king winks. Ha-ha, now that's cute. I feel so much better now.

The old steward schools his features and motions to a door a few steps away, walk the few feet, open the door, and look into the room. It takes my breath away. It's perfect. I feared it would have a princess appearance to it. However, it has a regal queenly aspect and has lots of dark colors and plant-life. I can live in here! I notice several doors one must lead to the king's room and one perhaps a dressing room along with the bathroom that Dagda told me about.

"Do you like it, or shall we find one you like, Rigan?" he asks.

"No, I want this room. Is it magic, handsome?" I say.

"Of course, little one it is and remade itself into what you'd like. I'm not surprised to spot a door leading to the garden. Feel free to ask your crows to stay there if you would like. I have an idea, beautiful..."

We are interrupted by servants who are flying through the room and one little light fairy who says, "My Goddess Consort Mor-Rigan, please follow me to the bath. I've made it with some spicy sandalwood for you, but if it's too much, I can change it."

I glance at Dagda who gives me a little peck on the cheek and says, "Go, beautiful and doll up for me. We can talk when you're ready. I'll come and escort you to the dining hall in high fashion."

I smile and go with the little fairy flying before me. When we get to the private bath, there's a sparkle, she changes to my size and bows a little as she introduces herself. "Goddess, I'm Flora. Ask me anything, and I'll do my best to answer or get you anything you need."

"Okay Flora, what about the best way to shut up the gossips... tonight?" I ask.

She giggles, "My lady, that's impossible, but we could make you as imposing as possible. That might scale the spite back some. They are especially careful if they fear it will expel them from the king's palace and out of his favor. Beautiful torque by the way. You can set it here on the vanity table while you bathe if you like."

I take off the precious gift and take a second and set it on the table. Then melting off my clothes I step into the bath. Oh, this is nice, just what I need after the battlefield. My mind thinks of the way I got here, but I hide the seething anger of my hatred for the invaders. I want to enjoy the bath then Flora's help as I get ready for what I'm sure will be a test at dinner. After she's helped me wash, she massages my whole body to the point I don't believe I can walk. I have to so when she finishes and taps my shoulder I sit up and walk on wobbly feet over to the vanity.

Flora reaches for me, "Please, Goddess pardon my touch."

"What, Flora, you touched every part of my nude body. I'm not offended, a little too relaxed, but not offended. Now let's get me ready. I'd like to impress the king."

"Well, you could do that the way you are now," she giggles as she lets go of me while I sit in front of a magic mirror. It is taking my image and flicking through different styles of hair and makeup. I catch one I like and point. Flora nods and raises an eyebrow.

"We are definitely going for over the top with that. I wholly approve," she says.

She makes me up, fixes my hair, dresses me, and brings out an ornate box covered in vines. She opens it, so it faces me, and I can glimpse what is inside. It's a twisted crown of silver hawthorn with twinkling sapphires all around it.

"I love this! Is it from Dagda?" I ask.

"Yes, ma'am, he said to tell you it would honor him if you would wear this as a symbol of his courtship. He'll ask you in person later."

I rub my hands together and say, "Yes, put it on me!"

Laughing she puts it on my head and surprises me by showing me a small dagger in a black sheath, slim and short. She secures the crown in place using it and more pins. We can still see the decorative tip of the little knife, but it's beautiful and belongs. I put on my torque and stand to glance into the mirror to decide if I'm happy with my appearance. What I observe is astounding. I'm head to toe in a black filmy dress that's so tight in places you can see everything. I recognize its tight, so it stays up and doesn't show even more. I look queenly the dark type, not the princess type. I'm thrilled. Too bad Bran isn't here. I feel a twinge of guilt because I'm so happy when I should be out getting revenge or grieving for him still. Last night I expect gave me some release. It's something that has changed me, and I'm more at ease. A knock at the door brings me out of my reverie. Flora gives me an appreciative nod and a questioning look.

I say, "Yes Flora, let's see if he's as happy as I am with his bad girlfriend." She opens the door slowly increasing the drama, then glances my way, so he follows her look.

His eyes widen, and he almost chokes. "Holy fucking vipers, Rigan. You look magnificent. I'm one lucky man. You are the most beautiful goddess I can remember in my lifetime." He reaches for me and I back away playfully.

"Oh, so it's that way, is it? Then the chase is on." He grins a sexy, cocky smile that says precisely what he's thinking. This should be fun. If he tears this dress off later, I'll let him. I'm happy he deems me beautiful.

"Believe me, handsome, I don't want my make-up messed... yet."

He gets my meaning and chuckles then sobers, "My beautiful, Rigan. Goddess of the forest, who brings life and death will you accept my hand and let me court you as a man who loves a woman?"

He's a good god for me. He lets me keep my love for his brother and understands me. I care for him. "I'll give you a chance to win my heart, my king... you are well on the way," I can't help myself and add, "any way you're good in the sack!"

He grins devilishly and holds his arm out for me to take. I place mine on top of his, and we walk out the door to the dining hall. The whole room is abuzz until we hit the doorway and wait as Tornitch introduces our presence.

"Dagda, the High King of Faery and his Phantom Queen Consort Mor-Rigan, rise and differ to your rulers," he booms. Everyone to a man stands and bows keeping their eyes to the floor as we pass to the head of the room. One brazen bitch looks up and stares a death look my way. I give her a slight lift of one side of my mouth in response. I'll be watching this one. I have to ask who she is later.

Dagda seats me on his right and kisses my hand before he sits in his chair beside me. I feel just a little like my old self and look through my lashes and mouth... fuck me. He knocks into the table and spills a cup of water in response. I love I'm having that effect on him.

He raises his hand in the air and moves in a circular motion for the crowd to resume their activities. The servants have the liquid cleaned up magically. It didn't even take a second, but it was worth it, and one of them is watching me with an interesting look. Careful. Glancing around the room he isn't the only one appreciating the view. I mark a few. It's to be expected, I haven't been in the court in a long time and never dressed to impress.

I pick out conversations and hear a repeat of the comment from earlier about my torque and what gall I have flaunting it in front of the king. Another says they wonder if it has a magic of its own is why I continue to wear it. Yet another says I wonder how long she'll have his favor. Well now, I know that answer... as long as I want it. But my torque does need some magic so I smooth my hand over it and whisper a little spell.

I have a lot of energy and am wide awake but not starving. I eat a little but drink more. The wine is strong, and I can tell my inhibitions are slipping. I lean close to Dagda and ask, "Hey big man, could we go dancing in the garden? I'm tired of the of the crowd people in here."

He smiles, stands taking my hand, and leads me out of the now quiet room.

When we reach the garden that Dagda had shown me earlier. He leads me to a paved patio and spins me then snaps his fingers, and his harp is in his hands. He plays for me and sings me a song that has me thinking I might stay here for a long while. Then he sets the harp down and commands it to play while we dance in the moonlight.

17

THE POOL

*T*he sunshine wakes me from my sleep. I'm in my room and Dagda is beside me snoring softly. Touching his face, I kiss him lightly before getting out of bed. I reach for a midnight blue robe that's been placed on the end of the bed and cover myself on my way to the bathroom. When I finish getting ready for my day and walk back into the room, Tornitch is there talking with my king. Dagda is sitting at a table eating and making plans for the day. I get it. Running a kingdom is work and requires considerable time. He reaches for my hand I hold on to his and sit beside him hungry myself. I fill my plate, and we plan our day. I'll be alone without my handsome god until evening it seems.

"Will that be all right Rigan or shall I take the day off and show you around the palace?"

"No, I think I'll be fine. Can I come to you if I want to see you though?" I ask. I'm not weak by any stretch and hate I the trepidation I feel being without him. I'll get over it if I have to force myself.

"Yes, you are always welcome. I'll be addressing issues

with some petitioners, and you can always be there and even help if you'd like to. In fact, that would take some of the boredom away from the petty arguments that sometimes are presented to litigate."

"No, I'm not quite comfortable enough to be in that kind of position here. I'd like to roam around if you don't mind."

"Do whatever you want, and I'll see you at dinner. I need to get ready and meet the masses," he says and kisses me. He licks my lips thinking he'll get away with teasing me, but I'm not letting him get away with that and bite his bottom lip. His eyes turn black as his pupils dilate with desire. Oh, that is enough. I see what makes me happy so turn him loose with a laugh.

He says, "Or, I could stay."

"Shew, get out of here and have fun at your king work. I'll see you later," I return, and he's gone.

Flora shows up out of thin air to help me get ready for my day while another maid called Janie clears away the breakfast. "Flora, how is your day." It surprises her that I ask I can tell. This will change for the ones who are helping me.

"My Phantom Queen, I... um I..."

Her face has fallen. Something is wrong. I say, "What it is? Tell me I encourage and take her hand the way Dagda does to make me feel more comfortable.

"Well... it's just... my little brother is ill, and my mother is gathering herbs to help him. I left him alone and feel terrible about it. It frustrates me that I can't help him," she blurts out.

"I can dress, have for a long time, Flora. You go home and watch your brother. If you want to come back later, you can. If not, I'll be just fine, and I'll know where you are if I get desperate."

Flora answers, "Thank you so much, my lady! She even hugs me, but I can't help thinking I missed something as she leaves.

When I'm dressed in my regular leather attire just a little more courtly. I take off to the kitchen. It is a beautiful kitchen and busy. I want to ask the cooks if they will make Dagda a dessert from me tonight with apples. One worker looks up at me and tells me I need to leave when he recognizes me and stops.

"How can I help you, Phantom Queen?" he asks.

"I want to request a special dessert for the king if you don't mind. Um, what is your name if you don't mind?"

The cook smiles when I ask. "I'm Joey," he answers, "and I'll make anything you ask... if I have the ingredients, Goddess. There are plenty of apples, my lady."

He points to a stool for me to sit on and hands me a plate of cookies dusted with sugar and a cup of milk then sits beside me while I explain what I'd like made. It is just a crispy dumpling, but I want to do something nice for Dagda. "Joey, will you please put a heart on it for me?"

He nods and smiles, "Yes, I will, my lady. Now, is there anything else I can do for you, Your Highness?"

"Will you point me in the way of the nearest exit? I need some time outdoors," I ask.

He walks with me to the door and warns, "It isn't always safe outside my lady, Artis, go with our lady and if there's even a speck of trouble get help."

Artis is a small stringy boy with curly dark hair that hangs to his shoulders. He bobs his head and takes hold of my hand. We stroll until we get closer to the trees then he pulls me to a path and into the woods. I go willingly. He changes into a stickman and runs, so I turn into my wolf and run with him. When we get to a pool of still dark water, he stops. He hasn't said one word, but I know he means well and has brought me to a special place. The little shy smiling face pierces my heart as he looks at me, he raises a hand and indicates that I should look at the pool.

It's so still, I can see our reflections in the water's darkness. Wait, what is this? I notice more images. A beautiful black panther. I concentrate, and the picture becomes clearer. There's a fight and a woman killing men who are terrorizing people who are hiding behind her. I say men, but they are Fomorian monsters I can tell the human looking ones by the way they are dressed. The others are monsters and easy to recognize. The warrior woman licks her sword when she's killed all of the criminals and looks up at me. I jerk back! It's me.

The vision is gone, and Artis is looking at me and says with understanding beyond his years, "It's a gift, and I hope you comprehend that you don't have to say goodbye... you're coming back. Some things must happen in the web of the world, mother."

Tears fall, I grab the boy and hug him. It has been too long since someone has seen the mother in me. He's right. I have something that needs to be finished. I know now that, I'll talk to Dagda tonight, so he knows that it's a mission I must complete, and I'll return to him. I'll make sure he knows that he's important to me.

Artis smiles at me, and we walk on, hand in hand, laughing and running in the woods. The time has gotten away, and it's time we get back to the palace, and time to get ready for the dinner the cooks have prepared for the court.

18

IT IS MISSING

I take a bath then get ready. Flora never shows up, so I dress. When I go to put on my torque that I'd forgotten to wear on my trip to the woods, it isn't on my table. Panicking I search the floor and the surrounding area. It isn't anywhere I tear my room apart looking for it, but it isn't here. I stop and take a deep breath to calm down and think for a minute. Now, what was I doing when I had it last. I was getting ready for bed and put it on my table. I never put it on this morning. Not thinking this morning, I was concerned with Flora, and I forgot... Flora. Where is the wench? I knew something wasn't right. Why didn't I go with my gut and figure out what was really her problem? Just as I'm deciding on recourse, Dagda saunters into my room with a little knock on the door facing and a smile for me.

"What, what is it? Did someone hurt you?"

Oh, that makes me feel a little better but not enough to quell my anger. Dagda, someone robbed me. I think Flora took my golden torque. The one that Bran gave me. I put a spell on it. It'll make anyone who touched it tell the truth when asked questions. At least I think it will, that is how I spelled it, but I didn't test it to be sure."

He never doubts me; instead he turns and bellows, "Tornitch!"

When the king's man enters he knows something has happened and asks, "Your Majesty, what do I need to do?" He waits for instructions with rapt attention.

Dagda orders, "The maid Flora, where is she man? We have cause to believe that she stole Rigan's gold torque. I need her brought to the throne room as quickly as possible, meet us there when you find her." Dagda takes my hand, and we leave to wait for the thief.

Pacing isn't making the waiting any more comfortable. There's a commotion in the hallway, and we look that way at the same time to see palace guards enter with a dirty and squirming Flora carried between two of them. She's yelling. There is a stream of blood dried on her chin where it's been cut. I don't even feel sorry for her; she looks to be fine otherwise.

I walk up to them, and the guards stop with their prisoner held firmly. I glare into her face and demand, "What have you done with my torque, Flora?"

She stops and calms, a haze covers her eyes, she answers, "I wanted to see if it would heal my brother, so I took it home and placed it on him. Nothing happened, and I was upset and didn't want to be caught with it, so I gave it to my lover. He'll sell it, so we can get away from the palace intrigue and selfish royals. We want a life of our own. You understand, don't you?"

"Who is your lover?"

"Torin, he works in the stables."

The drugged appearance leaves her visage and wide-eyed she cries recognizing that she's in trouble, and so is her lover. The king jerks his head to another guard, and he leaves to apprehend Flora's lover.

Dagda says, "Flora, all you had to do was to ask, and I would have taken the harp and seen to it your brother was healed. Why would you steal from the Queen Consort?

The crying prisoner answers, "Because she has everything, and I have nothing. There is no reason for her to miss the torque; it's only one of the many pieces of jewelry she has. I didn't think she would even notice it was gone. I deserve to have a life too."

"Not at the expense of the Phantom Queen Mor-Rigan. Now you'll face the penalty for your crime." He looks to his guards and orders, "Take her to the cells and keep her there until I decide on a punishment."

The guards leave and take the maid with them. Dagda gathers me close hugging me then we sit and talk waiting only minutes when the guards return with a man. One guard hands a cloth bundle to the king and backs away with a bow. Dagda opens it and within is my torque. He gives it to me, and I put it on vowing not to remove it again. I'm so relieved that I'm weak and my muscles jelly. I lean into my handsome god for support.

Neither of us address the man. The king orders them to take him to the cells with his lover until later when he can think better what he wants for them. Punishment is in order, but he wants to think clearer and not be too harsh. It would cause inner turmoil in the courts. No need making enemies. He has enough of those as it is, this could spark a more significant problem if not dealt with appropriately. Every court has its people who vie for power and the throne; this court is no different. It isn't as prevalent as human courts because most understand the power that Dagda wields, but they are still there in the shadows waiting for an opportunity to incite a takeover.

"Come, Rigan, let's go to my room, and I'll have something brought to us there. We don't need to go to dinner in the hall tonight."

I nod, and we go to his rooms and spend the night there. I forget to tell him about the black pool of prophecy and remember when he is snoring beside me in the dark. I'll tell him tomorrow I think falling into sleep myself. My dreams are all of revenge, and then I hear my druids call.

19

A NEW PLAN

I wake with a start and reach for my clothes. I need to leave now! My druids need me. Dagda is up already and, on the patio, eating fruit. Tornitch is handing him a cup of hot tea when I enter the area. The caring steward pours me a cup and leaves.

I sit and say, "I received a call from my druids, Dagda. I need to leave, but I must tell you something I saw yesterday." It's about Artis taking me to the pool and what I viewed. I describe everything even adding what the boy told me. "This is just the beginning Dagda. I'll return as fast as I can but get ready it might take a while. Is there a way you could go with me?"

There's pain on Dagda's face as he says, "I can't go, Rigan. There are plots against us. I have information come to me that someone here is planning to take your life, because of what happened with Flora and Tirn. Maybe when you leave, I can find out who is planning your downfall and kill them. Then when you get back, it'll be safe. I'll send as many guards with you as you need. Promise me you'll return. If you won't then, I'll let this kingdom crumble to shit and not think twice about it. I'd rather be with you than take a chance on never seeing you again."

"No, handsome. That won't be necessary. Please, find the plotters and make it safer here. Take care of the kingdom, I'll return. You have my word," I promise.

I'll come to you as soon as I take care of this problem. In fact," he walks over to a table, takes a stone from a drawer, and hands it to me. It's flat and has a perfectly worn hole in the middle. "Look into the hole, love" I do as he asks, and I see him sitting looking my direction. I look up at him as he continues, "At least with this stone, you can see where I am, you'll hear me too. I'll hear and see you too there's an image as soon as you look into the rock. Look into it at least once a day, and you'll see and know when I finish here, and I'm coming to you."

I can't wait. The pull of the druid's need is making me antsy, and I have to leave. He walks me to the front doors of the palace. I bend and kiss him goodbye. He crushes me to him kissing me hard, his hands in my hair. When he lets go the longing in his eyes has me wishing I could stay. I can't stay though and back away with a smile. "I'll be back as soon as I can my handsome love." Now he knows that I do love him, and it'll make the wait easier knowing I do. I turn and leave shooting through the doors and into the woods as fast as I can before I decide to stay.

I change into my crow and caw calling to my crows until they are all with me. Finn is beside me, and we fly to the Forest of Rigan as fast as we can. I should find a spell that can transport us more quickly...

It isn't long after we exit Faery that see my druids in the same open area where I told them the answer to the battle between the tribes. I caw to the others to cover me for a grand entry. They are so good at this. I burst from the black cloud of birds as my feet touch the earth in front of the druids. They have been waiting but are still shocked at my sudden arrival and bow before me.

"Thank you, you are too kind. Now, get up and tell me why have you called me out of Faery?" Looking up I notice Finn is perched on a limb above me. He is such a gift.

Gearoid stands and starts, "My Queen, we have a problem you need to know about. We can kill some intruders but need to be sure that is your will. We aren't warriors and killing isn't what we do well. If you don't want them killed what should we do about them?"

"Tell me the whole story, Gearoid, "I nod for him to continue.

Cian brings me a cover, so I can sit.

When I do Gearoid says, "Goddess, some Fomorians from the battle who escaped killing have been in the villages across the island. They are a bloody terror. A group of them have incited some people, and they are becoming an army. They travel from village to village and demand treasure saying they will return every month for more. They take what the treasure the villages have along with most of the food and leave doing the same to the next village. The next village on their route is Torn. We know you want to be there for your people, Rigan. We need direction and aren't sure what to do now. Will you instruct us?"

"Gearoid, you're right. This is the plan... "I lay out a plan and order Cian and Sorcha to run to the tribes and see what support we can garner for this enterprise. In a day, we'll surround the village of Torn and sit and wait until the enemy is there. We'll strike and not let a single one live. I need to rest. I move over to the edge of the clearing and change into a hawthorn. I need to be still. The trees around me whisper to me calming my fighting spirit as I look into the streams of possible futures to choose the one that will be best for my people. I sink in deeper and watch then rest. I can hear the druids now that I have decided on the best future. Listening to them talk I understand that Cian is back and has contacted Zander and Tomas and they can have their armies here by noon tomorrow. I look into the streams of time once more to be sure this path is right. It's the best outcome that we kill all the errant Fomorians. My way isn't always the best. I check each of their futures and am hurt when I see that we also must sacrifice. I'll try to help with that but not enough to warp the chosen future.

Sorcha has shown up and is giving her report to Gearoid. It seems that the tribes are all aligned for once. I'm glad they are and relax while the surrounding trees sing me to sleep.

20

NO ONE LIVES

I fly up into the branches where Finn is perched, and he tells me telepathically what the crows have all seen. The Fomorian renegades are well on their way to Torn. They will arrive just before dark. He knows my plans, I'll be with the humans for the fight in my wolf form.

"I need the crows to watch and warn me if things change. Finn, if you'll watch me fight and warn me if someone tries to surprise me from behind. Is that all right with you?"

"I'll do that, Rigan. Are you sure you don't want me on the ground with the humans?"

"What? And take a chance on you getting hurt! I couldn't stand it. Please... I need to fight without worrying that someone will bash me from behind. I trust you, and it'll make me able to fight better knowing you're watching."

"I always want to make it easy for you to fight. I'm glad you trust me. Do you think I'm weak and can't fight?"

"Oh, that isn't what I think, not at all. Sorry, Finn. How about you fight with me as soon as the killing starts, back to back then?"

"I like this plan much better, and I bet Dagda would too. You might shoot him a message. Just to put him at ease."

"I'll do that just as soon as I figure out how to be easy about it."

For the rest of the afternoon, the druids spell the woods to conceal us until we're ready to show ourselves to the enemy. The chieftains, Zander and Tomas are here and greet us. We share our plan with them. They agree but ask if they and their men can rush the invaders first. I take a second to view my vision of the future, and it's a better outcome and agree to the idea. The tribe's soldiers are proud of the fact they will protect the goddess, and it has built them up and added confidence. It appears I have an army again.

NIGHT HAS FALLEN. I watch from the trees with my small militia. They are silent and move with stealth. The Forest of Rigan covers any noise they make that would alert the enemy. I almost bolt from my hiding place when a Fomorian strikes Eimer, my druid healer a slap to her face. The scum is yelling at her and trying to force her to use magic to heal one of his men who is lying on the ground in front of them. Finn holds me back and motions with his head that she has this under control. The protector in me isn't happy, but he's right. She looks over the wounded man. He is beyond her abilities and will die anyway, but she takes gentle care of him in his last moments the same way she does for the villagers and all who seek her help. It's the druid way.

The same ass who hit her is shouting orders for someone to take the children and herd them away from the adults. Okay, that's all I can stand when one of them rips the new baby I delivered only days ago from Eva's arms. I trill a signal to the others and pull Finn with me as I rush the jerk screaming at the top of my lungs, "No one lives!"

So much for letting the chieftains charge in first. They are beside me anyhow, yelling, "For the Phantom Queen!"

I take the squalling baby as Finn punches the dirtbag in the throat with a killer punch over my head. I place the little girl in Eva's hands and tell her to take all the children and hide in the trees with the druids. They and the forest will protect them. The druids aren't always fighters, but they can perform spells to help in battle. Like the mist, they are raising to confuse the enemy. They will help heal the wounded and help when the struggle is over. They are excellent leaders.

The battle is on! I can't wait and shift. Finn is right with me in his human form at my side. He has a sword and is stabbing the asshole I took the babe from, to finish him. I'm confident he can keep my back safe so start on my own killing when an enemy thinks he can take Finn from behind. He stabs at me, I lunge at him and bite into his face then tear it off with as much power as I have. He's dead when he hits the ground. My crows flutter and fly through the fighting screeching and scratching. The battle rages around me. As soon as I kill one, another takes his place, but it doesn't last. There aren't many, not even a hundred. I have no mercy and destroy all I meet. I'm lost in a berserker vision when Finn touches me I growl before I see it's him and back off.

He hisses, "Bloody hell, Rigan, you can stop now they're all dead."

I look down at the pile of dead at my feet. He and I are standing in front of several bodies mangled beyond belief. I smile, "I guess I *can* stop now. Is there at least one to question?"

"No enemy is left alive. A few shifted and ran away. We'll track them tomorrow. Tonight, we need to dispose of the dead and help the villagers clean up this bloody mess. Unless you have a better plan, goddess."

"You're right let's help the villagers. Where are they anyway?" I glance around and see them poking heads out around trees. I wave a hand to my druids. They come, and I command, "Spell the area so that the villagers aren't disturbed by the condition of the bodies lying around their village. I want them to see and learn a lesson of battle. I don't want them hurt mentally from the carnage."

"Yes, Mor-Rigan," Gearoid says then he and the druids do that very thing.

Zander and Tomas come toward me, and I reach them shaking their hands. "Thank you both. I owe you and intend to bless you and each of your villages."

"You're welcome, Phantom Queen. I'll welcome any blessings you bestow on my people, but there are some enemy still on the island. Several here ran away," says Zander.

Tomas agreeing, and nodding adds, "We'll help you track them in the morning. That is if you're going after them. We will even if you don't they are causing trouble everywhere they go. We've heard all kinds of tales, some are even true."

I grin at them and their eagerness. They are my men. "Let's get Torn settled then I'll take you up on that," I say, then walk to the woods straight to Eva. The baby is asleep, and her sons stand around her watching as I walk over.

They all look over as Mac comes riding into the gathering. Enbarr pulling his chariot. He has a smile on his face when he says, "So more fun, Rigan? I thought you had enough by now." He hops over one of the large wheels showing off coming toward us and scoops me up in a hug. I hug him back feeling grimy to his clean ocean scent.

I let it go and punch him in the arm teasing, "I won't have enough until all the invaders are in their graves and we have ferried them to the Otherworld. In fact, I'm letting my crows feast on the bodies of the dead, but what about you helping me take these dead right now?"

"I can't do that," he says with all seriousness. I give him a look questioning with a raised eyebrow.

Mac bursts out laughing, "I just wanted to see what your reaction would be, Rigan. Of course, I'll help."

Tomas laughs and pats Mac on the shoulder as he turns to leave. He says, "I'll talk to you in the morning, goddess. We can plan our tracking strategy then." Zander nods and walks off with him. I'm delighted to see those two so friendly.

I take Mac's hand and look into his blue depths. He nods, and we raise our clasped hands and wave a gathering motion with our other hands. The spirits around us float up in a group and wait until Mac says, "You dead shall have the honor of repaying your debt to us and our island by serving the Phantom Queen in her dark army of the dead. I curse you, you are unable to move to the other heavens until she releases you... if ever."

I shift to a dark Phantom Queen appearance before their eyes. My hair blowing behind me gives them a clear vision of my blood-red eyes and horns. They all bow at once. Mac sends a jagged bolt of lightning across the sky for emphasis. I give him an evil grin. He's so good to me!

"I accept your fealty. Come, we are going to your final resting place."

Mac and I swirl magic around them and take them to the other world. We spot, standing before the entrance to the place my darkling army lives, a waiting Bran. He's my general he felt us bringing him recruits. As we get nearer, the souls of the dead are sucked into the dark void that the living can't enter. I smile at Bran remembering our time together with Dagda. He does, and his eyes shine in the dark. His lips are on mine. In this place, he is a spirit, but I still feel the tingle and want builds in my center.

Mac says, "All right you two should I create a room from the aether?"

Bran laughs and says, "If only it were so easy, friend. I'll take care of the army brother. Rigan, call on me soon. I can only be out of the dark heaven of the army for minutes. It is a strain, I need to go back. I love you." He presses a kiss to my head and is gone, dissolved like a mist that feels like a breeze.

Mac takes my hand in his large one and with a thought returns us to Torn where the druids have everything well in hand.

21

THE TEST

$\mathcal{T}$he sun is high, and the village is bustling as the people get to work like it's a regular workday. There is a sense of happiness. It seems their mental health is intact my druids did well with the spell I asked for after the battle. I stand with my back against a tree watching them work. We made plans with the tribal leaders and will be on our way to hunt all invaders who have bad intentions on our island. Mac is still here and walks up to give me his goodbyes.

"Rigan, I have a report from my sea creatures that there's another ship of Fomorians headed for our shores. I'll let you know when they are ready to land. It'll be a day at least for them to land. I'll send you a message before then."

"Thank you, Mac. I'll find the ones who evaded us last night and head to the seashore." I give him a hug. "And thank you for always being here for me.

He doesn't give me a chance to say no when he pressed me back into the tree and kisses lips passionately. I kiss him back melting into him. His large hands brush my face as he backs away. I can't breathe and let him back up, but I don't want to. I check my feelings, is this because I feel so bereft leaving Bran? No, I have always loved Mac since I was a little girl. I always thought he wasn't interested in me and took the next best option... friendship. Is he... interested?

"I'll talk to Dagda. But know this, Rigan we've been friends for long enough. I've wanted you for a long time, but I knew my place. Now I want to change that. If you don't want me, tell me now."

"I do want you," I whisper, "are you sure? I don't share well, I want you too but don't want you to have other goddesses. If you want someone else tell me so we can part and remain friends. The truth is if I catch you unfaithful, you will never be my friend again. I'll avoid any and all contact with you. I know that isn't fair when I have your brothers, but that's what I can handle. Do you still want me knowing this?"

A giant smile breaks his face, and he answers, "Yes, I'm sure. I know you well and know how you operate, love. And I've changed my mind. I'm coming with you on this campaign. I can get messages from the sea from Dord."

Thinking about him and wanting him will not be easy. I'll be glancing his way until I have him in my bed. "Well, great! Now that will be a test."

He gives me a sly grin and says, "You think it'll be hard for you..."

"It better be hard for me." I put a hand on his hard stomach, and he groans.

"We better get going the others will be waiting," I say. It takes every bit of willpower in my body to walk away from the tree.

Eimer sees us and motions. I turn from my intended

route to see what she needs. Mac nods to me and continues over to Zander and Tomas who are waiting.

Eimer says, "Goddess, thank you for saving the village. We have a gift for you." She hands me a thick red ribbon that has a gold pattern woven into the sides. The design looks like little crows with a wolf every few inches. It's long enough that I can tie it at my waist, but I think I want it sewn on the hood of one of my cloaks. This must have taken a while to make. They have been planning this gift, and I love it.

My eyes water and I hug Eimer and say, "Please tell the villagers how happy I am to have this. I love it and the thought. I have to get going, or the invaders who escaped will terrorize other villages."

She smiles at me happy that I accepted the gift. I wind up my pretty, place it in my pocket, and walk to the army waiting for me. Mac motions for me to step up into the carriage with him. It is so tall I have to hop to get in. I almost shifted but didn't fumble, so I stayed in my human shape and waved to the villagers of Torn as we rolled by. They are bowing but with smiles not fear.

We might have gone only a few hundred yards when a tracker finds the signs of the criminals we're searching for, and there's blood in the tracks. I'm hoping that means they will die without our help. The Huntsman moves out ahead of us, and we continue until it is dark.

My stomach is grumbling but not for long because the tribesmen have camp followers who have our meals cooked. After accepting a plate, I wolf it down. Mac watches and offers his to me... that makes me smile. Taking a fake swing at his arm, I say, "No, you're a growing boy, and I need you strong for what I have planned... as soon as we can, that is."

After we've all eaten, we sit around a fire, and I'm handed

a cup of honey mead. Thanking the young one who gave it to me I start, "Finn, did you and the crows see any of the invaders from the sky today."

"We did Goddess, and some have already passed from this plain. The sea god has moved them on to the Otherworld. There are still some left; we are still hunting."

"Where was I when this happened?" I wonder.

"Well the killing was easily done by the tribesmen at midday and when you needed a break... for... well, you know, Mac Lir did us the honor of moving them on. We have you back, Rigan. Do you need me because there is a saucy wench I want to show something?" He grins at me, and I roll my eyes and shew him away laughing.

Tomas sits across the fire from me and says, "It wasn't hard, or we would have called you, Phantom Queen," he chuckles at his joke.

"I see how it is... be warned, I'll return the favor sometime when you least expect it heathen. I have to sleep, so I'm turning in just remember... when you least expect it."

Everyone gets a good laugh as he pretends to be scared. Mac and I move off to a place prepared for us on the ground near a smaller fire. It's a little cold tonight, and I'll enjoy Mac's warmth. First, though, I need to talk to Dagda and tell him I'm taking another lover. He deserves respect, and I promised him honesty. Mac walks away to give us some privacy. I take out the rock with the hole in it and look into it, sure enough, like my handsome king told me I can see him. I wonder if he can hear me so far away, so I say, "Dagda, I miss you."

He searches for me. It looks like he sees me, he smiles and says, "My beautiful Queen Consort, I miss you too and am glad you're safe. How is the eradication going?" He leans forward in his chair and squints his eyes looking at me closer.

"It's gone well, we protected the village of Torn from the marauders. A few did slink away, and we're tracking them. It may be a while until we find them, we've already killed a few more. I'm safe. Are you able to come to me or still battling the political side of the Faery kingdom?"

He has a look of guilt on his face as he answers, "I wish I could my love, but I've found a bigger plot. As soon as I take care of it, I'll be with you."

"I'll be waiting for you. I have to ask you something if you say no I'll understand, but I don't think you will, or I wouldn't ask."

"Ask me anything, Rigan."

"Okay, Mac has asked me to be his lover... "I wait, and so does he, "I would like to say yes, but I won't if you don't like it. I want nothing to come between us. What do you think?"

"It has been this way with the gods and goddesses for as long as I can remember, Rigan. I'm glad that you're asking me first. Is my brother with you now?"

"He's close, I'll call him over." I wave and say, "Mac, Dagda wants to speak with you." I hand him the rock, and he looks into it and says nothing for several minutes.

Then he says, "Yes, brother I understand, and I promise." He hands the rock back his face stoney. I don't have a clue what just happened.

With my heart in my throat, I look into the hole and Dagda says, "Rigan, I'm so happy you kept our deal and are honest with me. This is still what I want, honesty and your love. I didn't hold back with Bran, and I accept Mac. I told him the rules, and he's agreed. Honesty, no other women, if he hurts you, I'll kill him, and he can find his own way to the afterlife."

"Oh Dagda, I wish you and Bran were both here with me."

"So, do I beautiful, so do I. Take solace with Mac Lir and find me tomorrow night, so I know you're safe."

"I will, dream about me, love." He winks at me, and I put my stone away. I'm glad that went well, but it's time to sleep. Mac comes back, and we snuggle together.

I can't sleep this way... I've wanted this for as long as I can remember, others are here, and we have no privacy. I wonder... I look up into Mac's face, and he's staring at me back, I guess he can't sleep either. I put my finger to my lips and shh quietly then put the same hand on his chest and raise up and kiss him. He lets me know he wants my mouth open by moving his tongue over my lips. His mouth tastes good and a little like mead. I moan into it and catch myself, being quiet will not be easy. I have wanted him forever. He deepens the kiss and rolls over putting his hands under me and grinds his pelvis to my all too ready center. I push back up into him. I can't do it! I push him back, get up, and curl a finger in a come-hither motion. No one is awake but us as we run into the woods. He has our blankets and his cloak and puts them on the ground in front of a large oak. Then stands there waiting for me.

I say, "Take off your clothes. I have wanted to see you for a very long time, and I want a long look."

He melts the clothes from his beautiful muscles. His cock standing straight and hard in his excitement.

"Even better than I imagined," I coo and move toward him.

"You imagined? I want to see you too, little crow," he says, his voice husky with need.

I back up a step and melt off my clothes but slowly. When I finish, he is all but panting. I can't wait and won't make him either. I push him to the tree and let my hands touch every part of him then I sink down to my knees and take his hard dick in my mouth. He's large, so I use my hand pumping as I move on him. He runs his body in motion with me making it easy for me, but he's gentle and doesn't shove the way I've known some to do when I was younger. I better stop before it is too late. He's holding on and not coming though. I stand and kiss him, and he kisses me back lifting me to him. He lays me on the blankets, and his hands are inside me with ease, I'm so wet. I guide him to my wet slit.

He whispers, "So impatient."

"Yes, hurry."

He does and is inside me, I pump back with my own thrusts. Then he just stops... what... I was almost there... then... he flips me over on my hands and knees kneeling behind me he holds me up with one arm and enters me again. Oh, the stretch! He's deeper, and I'm going to come fast! This feels so good. He pumps hard, and I come in minutes. I don't even try to be quiet anymore and scream, "I'm coming, Mac."

Then he is coming too and telling me the same thing. We collapse on the blanket and sleep.

22

MORE FIGHTING

I wake in just a few hours. It's still dark but the moon is bright and orange. I turn in Mac's arms. What was that? I think I see movement in the shadows. Following the motion, I tap on Mac's arm that's around me. He's awake and tightens his hold on me for a minute then silently is on his feet squatting and moving into the trees hauling me with him under his cloak of invisibility. With hand motions, he tells me that he sees only four forms sneaking around. He reaches around and Fragrach, his sword, is in his hands. I know he hates to kill, but I also know he will if he needs to defend me... well any of us in the camp. In the dark, he drops the cloak, and with one look he points to the field where there are more of the dark forms.

A tap on my shoulder and I just about jump out of my skin. Tomas is looking at me with an embarrassed crooked grin. He motions, telling me to shift and he'll rush the shadows and yell to wake the camp. We understand, and I sink into my wolf. I smell the intruders so much that I know exactly where they are with my extended senses.

Tomas takes off, Mac is with him, and I go straight for the nearest dark form. The moon shines on it, it's a goblin. In fact, they are all goblins. I close my eyes when the screech of the banshee's call cuts through the night. An ugly little toad pops up in front of me and takes a swing with a broad-bladed ax. I dodge and jump on him. He goes down with my weight but is fighting like the dickens. Adrenaline surges though me and I squirm out of the ugly runts hold clawing every part of him I can manage. I rip his neck and nick an artery, he's a goner. Mac is beside me and stabs him to end his suffering. Helping is more his speed anyway. I love him that way. I understand how he feels and am happy he's protecting me despite the way he thinks about killing. This being friends before starting a deeper relationship has merit. I have deep feelings for Mac, he has for me as well, especially for him to kill for me.

Tomas shouts so loud that most of the camp who weren't awake from the banshee's call is now up joining the fight. Warriors enter the fight as soon as they are on their feet. The whole camp is buzzing with the battle. It only lasts for minutes, but the fighting is vicious. The enemy is overtaken, and they are dead at our feet. We've gotten used to the process of these battles now, and the tribesmen are starting the cleanup. The bodies are piled up and left for the crows. Mac ferries them to the otherworld. I find my sisters.

"Badb, I heard you call was there many who lost family tonight?" I ask.

"No sister but your young Zander lost a brother, his name is Ultan, and dear to the leader. Ferry him yourself to honor him. Macha and I will go to the tribal leader and give him what comfort we can while you're gone. It will make him feel better knowing it's you who carries his dear one to the otherworld. We'll be here when you return."

I turn to the camp and find Zander's brother's spirit waiting and wondering around the camp. Before I get to him, I spy his dead body and a gasping goblin close to him still living... not for long. I take my sword and stab him in the chest. Taking it out I lick the blood from the blade. My rage at our loss is fiery hot, and I want any enemy lurkers to see I relish their deaths. I want them to tell everyone they meet how vicious I am.

Calming some, I find the spirit I was searching for and make my body match his, so he can see me. This makes it, so the surrounding soldiers don't notice me any more than they see him. I reach for his hand, and he smiles at me taking it in his. "Phantom Queen, no one will answer me. I need to know how Zander is, did he survive the fighting? I can't find him."

"Yes, Ultan, he's safe, but morning his loss," I answer hoping it will sink in that he's the one who has passed the veil.

"Did he lose so many then? Not many die... oh it's me, isn't it? he says as he figures it out.

"Yes, but I'm here for you and will stay until you're in one of my favorite heavens. Let's go find some of your other family, shall we?" I ask.

I concentrate on his family, and I know just where they are. He has generations of family who are enjoying the heaven where they live now until they return. If they ever do everyone has a choice, but most return to a flesh body at least once. They keep all their memories until the second they breathe life again, and then they forget and become a new person. However, some can touch their old life in some way. I've seen some who live the same as they did in their previous life and some who are very different making up for mistakes. Ultan and I move through the aether until I get to a place with a large gate to a city. We enter, and it's like a party. A large gathering is waiting for him. When the Bean Sidhe calls it alerts family on both sides of the veil.

"Son, here! I'm here. Oh, my baby," says an older woman with silver hair running as fast as her little legs can carry her. When she reaches Ultan, she wraps him up and giggles, "I have missed you. Come, we have so much to catch up on." Still holding on to her son she turns to me and says, "Thank you Goddess Rigan for staying with him on his journey. I'm so happy he wasn't alone. You have honored us."

He faces me and says. "Yes, my Phantom Queen, thank you. You have been good to my family and me. Please, when you go back release the other soldiers and their families. Let them go home and live long lives. We have cleaned out most of the invaders already, and the tribes can defend themselves or call the gods when there is a problem. And if you don't mind, please comfort my brother and tell him I'm with mom and we're happy."

A tear runs down my cheek unchecked. I let go of my rage and look down as I brush the wetness away then say, "I intend to do just that Ultan, I'll tell your brother, but the living miss the dead very much. He might not be happy to hear the words, but I will tell him. I'll also tell him to look for you on Samhain."

He nods and walks away arm in arm with his mother, and they are actually talking about having tea! I smile at that and move through the aether back to the men.

23

SOME GO HOME

When I get back to camp, my sisters are with Zander. Macha stands to kiss me goodbye. Badb is right behind her with a kiss and they are on their way home. I raise a thick fog so misty that you can feel the wetness. I leave Zander, so he can have some time alone.

I need Mac. He sees me at the same time I do him. When he reaches me, he gathers me to his big chest. He knows intimately how hard escorting the dead can be.

"Mac, Ultan, Zander's brother asked me to stop this war. He is right, we have to end this and go home. Let's let the soldiers and their families go home. We can respond when there is a problem and not seek any more battles. Bran is avenged. I'm tired of fighting and don't want to see more of our people die too soon."

"You know that I hate the fighting. I agree whole-heartedly to getting you away from it. Come, let's call a war conference with the tribal chieftains... " he

leaves off short without finishing when Finn lands before us.

He reports, "In our scouting goddess, we've seen nothing in the area. There might be some giants in the mountains, but we haven't seen them in the open and only heard tales in some towns. There is no clear danger here that we have noticed Rigan."

"Thank you, Finn, I want to talk to the others then we want to disperse the army. We have all the revenge that Bran would stomach. Get some rest, and I'll see you later," I say.

"Goddess Mor-Rigan, I don't agree. This must be continued. We need to eradicate all the invaders from the island before we go home. This is how we'll keep the people safe," Zander insists.

"I understand how you feel, but there's no immediate threat, and I don't want to see any more of our people die. I told you that Ultan asked me to let you know that he's happy and with your mother."

"Please, goddess, that doesn't help. If one more person tells me he isn't suffering and happy now, I'll blow. He isn't here. I was supposed to protect him, and now you want to leave, and I won't get my revenge on his killers!"

I sit back in my seat. I understand and look into the waves of time hoping to see something that will make my answer for me and see nothing. Thinking for too long before I speak, he starts again.

"I'm sorry, goddess. I didn't mean to yell at you," he softly says rubbing his head and walking away. He sits in the farthest chair from all of us.

Now I have to speak. "I understand, Zander. How about a compromise?" He sits up listening. "Let's have the families and most of the soldiers go home. We can assemble a small group of our most trusted and unattached warriors to find the criminals who murdered your brother. Then we go home. Mac Lir will have to go and come back as the sea calls. He has to do his work also so that kingdom flourishes. I'll be with you for a while longer, but I also have a forest calling, druids, and villages who need my care."

His visage serious he stares into my eyes and says, "Perfect. It's a deal, Phantom Queen."

He sends his men to tell the army what we have decided. As I thought would happen many refuse to go. They have a purpose of caring for the land and its occupants. I agree with them.

I need to hear from Dagda, so I find a spot off by myself and pull out the stone he gave me. We talk for a very long time. I know Mac will be looking for me, but I want to know one more thing.

"Hey, love did you figure out a punishment for Flora and her lover yet? I've been thinking about it, and I don't want them hurt. Can you let them go?"

"Oh, you have a soft heart, beautiful. I did let them go and still made it look like punishment. I banished them together and made them leave the palace. Only a fool couldn't see that they love each other and were just trying for a life together."

"That's perfect. You are such a good person. I love you." I say knowing that I miss him with all my heart.

"I love you too. What is happening? I have to go little crow there is a commotion outside my door." He blows me a kiss and is gone.

By morning most of the camp is packed and leaving.

Happy for this to be over for them. Watching them go makes me long for Dagda even more. The talking through the rock isn't enough. I reach for Mac's hand, and he squeezes mine knowing how I feel.

24

HE LOVES ME

*I*t has been months since this bloody war stated, six to be exact. It's spring, and I want to be home before Beltane. I'm tired and going to leave this group, but I want them to go home and be safe. I don't want to worry that they have evolved into a lawless band of marauders terrorizing the countryside the way the invaders did what seems like so long ago.

Finn hands me a cup of honey mead as I sit at the morning fire with the group we have left. There are only a dozen or so not including my crows. They take care of themselves very well. How am I going to tell them what I'm worried about?

Zander pats my knee and says, "It is over isn't it, goddess Mor-Rigan?"

"Yes Zander, it is, and I want to go home. We have avenged our families, and the island is safe. There will always be a problem crop up, and we'll handle those as they come to us." No more did I get his out than the crows descend and flock over me.

"Okay, I take it back. The crows have sighted a ship full of Fomorians Mac. One of them landed on it and has overheard plans to ravage the island and take home all the gold and treasure they can find. Our fog had deterred all but this one ship of the enemy that was able to make it through.

But that's not all, there's another threat, much smaller. The giants the scouts thought might be in the hills, definitely are, and they are coming toward us. There are only three of them, and we should be able to kill them quickly. There are villages to the east they are moving toward. I think we should hurry and meet them as close to the mountains as possible. We can get there by nightfall.

Mac, can you send a storm to the sea and sink that ship, or do you have to be there?" Not sure why I don't know this... it's something we haven't ever needed to talk about though.

"I will have to be there. I'll travel as fast as I can and meet you on the mountains when the ship is sunk." He thinks for a minute and says, "I should stay then go later."

He gets to his feet, and I say, "I think we can handle the small force and only three giants. If you sink the ship, we won't have more invaders to hunt down." I get up too knowing he won't wait, and I want a private kiss goodbye. We walk to our tent, and there are no words as he lays me gently on the pallet we had just gotten up from. Our emotions are high, I feel tears leaking from my eyes and grind my forehead into his chest for comfort.

"Hold me just a minute I want to see if time will show me your fate, then when I see you're safe I want to kiss you so well you won't be able to get back to me fast enough."

He tightens his grip on me and rocks me while I look into the visions of the future. So much is not clear, but I do see that he sinks that ship, and none survive. Then I see a

Fomorian on a mountain, and he's asleep under a tree. His jet locks crusted with leaves he looks up as if he can see me I'm shocked by his crystal blue eyes. They are from my childhood visions, so light the way only gods' eyes look. It stands to reason; some gods and goddesses have Fomorian ancestry. I have no idea what this means. It's like many things I see. Only time will tell what the pictures really mean. As I live them, I understand. The vision dissolves, and I'm here in the arms of my love, Mac. I intend to keep my word. I reach for his face with both hands. A tickle in my center starts a throb. Why stop at a kiss? I press my lips to his and lick his lips, he opens his, and his tongue enters my mouth as he deepens the kiss.

I moan, "Mac, stay for a bit, please?"

He smiles and reaches to take off my clothes. I melt them away and start on his from my laying down position. I have to take a moment to admire his fine physique and run my hands over him. His stiff cock feels silky, but I can't wait and want him on top. He raises up to see me better. I wiggle for him, spread my legs, and rub my clit, now he knows that I like what I see this much. He likes it too if I don't miss my bet because he lowers himself over me again and kisses me deeply. My bear nipples hard from the chilly temperatures brush his muscular chest, and I purr at the feeling. He is grinding his hard cock into my clit almost pushing me over the edge. Then he stops and raises my ass on his legs pushing them up on his body. He watches me then says, "I want to see you come to remember the look until I return. Come for me, Rigan."

"I'm almost there now, sexy man. I groan softly as he enters me and leans down with his arms around my shoulders holding me close. Ah, he's so deep... I'm going to come fast... every movement is magic. He's watching my face with his hand in my hair. I can't help but close my eyes as my orgasm starts and I thrust in rhythm with him and come again before he stops. He backs up and lifts up on his knees, and I continue thrusting, so he can come. When he does, I know I won't forget his look either. He slumps over me on his arms as much of our skin touching as possible. I love the feeling, and I love how he loves me. I don't want him to go. Letting him will be hard. If I didn't have to, I would beg him to stay. He's snoring softly. I roll him over, so he can nap for a little while. He makes that sucking his tongue sound as he settles, and I smooth his soft hair away from his face as I sit back and let him sleep. The trip to the sea will be hard, and I want him rested.

WHEN MAC WAKES he's smiling, but I know it's to make it easier on me. He kisses me gently and says, "I'll be back as fast as possible, my love. Then we can start our new family life without having to use the stone to speak with Dagda."

I nod and stand on my toes to kiss him one last time before he goes. He blinks, and I can see all his love pour down onto me from his eyes. He does a little flip with his hand and hands me hands me a bracelet made of shells then he turns and leaves.

I put on my treasure. My heart literally hurts, and I don't turn from watching Mac until he is so far away and just a speck on the horizon.

Finn startles me when he lands in a flutter at my feet then shifts. "My lady you must come now."

We shift and fly. He leads me to an area at the base of the

mountains where there are three ugly giants. They are ugly and appear to have slime stuck everywhere on their horrid bodies. The smell is awful. I see that there are others with them the dirty Fomorians some look human. I wonder who is in charge. When one of the more human-shaped one's shouts, "Don't stop. I want to pillage the next village then go to the sea to meet our kinsmen coming for us. Kill everyone and take the food but make sure you get all the gold and any treasure they have."

I fly higher to make sure they are no more giants in the area. "Come on let's go back and tell the others where the giants are. We need to hurry they're making it to the village faster than we thought," I say.

25

THIS CHANGES THINGS

The camp is packed when we land. I tell Tomas and Zander what we've seen. The giants move quick and are headed to a village in their path if we don't hurry they'll get there before us. I shift into my wolf and lead our small but lethal force forward at a fast clip. I only stop at the edge of the village to verify my plan will still be the best path forward. I notice the giants have plundered the town, there are several dead lying in their own blood. One of the giants reaches for a small boy, and a man who was on the Fomorians side rushes forward. He isn't like the monsters.

He's beautiful to look at and shouts, "No, you've had enough. Now let the people go. Take the treasure and let's leave."

One of the slimy bastards answers, "Fuck you, Rian. You don't give the orders here. Croag does, what do you say I'm hungry and want this boy?" He faces a man who looks familiar to me. The others stop quietly behind me as they reach the area.

The ugly man is the one I'd seen giving orders earlier in

the day. He says, "Eat all you want Bork, but we leave in an hour."

When the giant reaches for the boy again, the beautiful Fomorian takes his sword and slices the fingers of the giant off. He evades the giant's furious thrust with his other hand that sports a sickle. But the giant has help, and they attack the man.

I can't wait and enter the fray. The defender isn't moving, and I need to help. My friends must have thought the same thing because we all rush them at the same time. My crows fly into the giants faces confusing them and give my group a few precious seconds to rush into the fight. The giants bat them out of the air, and many of them lay on the ground. I order them to back away until a better time. The Fomorians have beaten the man who saved the boy until he's a bloody pulp. While I watch to see if he is breathing, I'm hit with a sword in my shoulder and go down. I land beside the bleeding protector.

There is no Bean Sidhe call, so I know my sisters are not here warning of the death of a family member. Both good and bad news.

I try to flip myself over and jump up, but I can't move. There must be some kind of poison or magic on the sword, and I'm defenseless against the blows raining down on me. All I can see is the dark headed beautiful Fomorian on the ground beside me. I try to shift, and that isn't working either. The dark man reaches for me and pulls me under his body surrounding me with his. I black out from the pain but only for seconds. Now, they aren't hitting me anymore... the pounding his body is taking for me is terrible. I don't think he can stay alive much longer. He is at the moment. If I could, I would use my magic to heal him.

The poison prevents me from doing anything at all. I can tell the fight is over because the sounds of battle have quieted.

I listen and hear Croag giving orders, "Lock up the prisoners in the village supply shed."

They have taken all the food out of the room, shove us in, close the doors, and slam the latch in place. It couldn't hold us if we could move. It's only a grass hut typical to the hill folk. I'm useless, and none of us are moving. I know that they put the traitor to their cause in here with us because he's beside me. There's no one to ask to keep watch, wait, my crows are squeezing in through a crack in the wall where the frame is warped. If I could just move... I'd have us out of here by removing some grass off of the hut and sneaking out. One of my birds sits on my chest and snuggles down. I should rest for a while. I can't move. It might be a good idea to relax and let my crows guard us.

I let go and drift. While I sleep my body is healing itself but even asleep, I can tell it's cold. If I think it's cold, the men with me must be freezing. These Fomorians will pay. I had no reason to continue this fight until now, but the rage has risen again. The minute I can move, I'll make them pay. That is the last thought I have as I find my rest. I'm warm. The beautiful now scarred and bloody Fomorian has once again wrapped me in his arms. I test to see if I can move and I can.

I say, "Thank you for your protection." My crows walk around the hut waking the others who can also move now. I get up making no noise and ask, "I can heal you will you let me repay you this way?"

He groans, "Yes, please, then I'll help you escape the Fomorians. I don't agree with what they have done to the people of your island. Our kin sent us to find open land for migration, not to conquer and steal. I want no part of the monsters who brought me here. Will you let me join you?"

I reach for him and touch him on his chest. He looks straight into my eyes. I see no lies in them. I close mine and concentrate. Warm healing magic flows. It makes me happy to see him better when I open my eyes, but he still has a long scar on his face that the magic didn't take away. It doesn't take away from his looks, in fact, it makes him even more handsome. Embarrassed by my thoughts, I move on to my men who are also in need of healing.

"Okay, who is next?" I ask.

Finn says, "My lady, Tomas is the worst." I creep to him and see that he has a deep wound in his leg. I take a while, but he's up with no limp when I finish. I turn to Finn, and he has the others lined up in order of need. When I heal the last man, I'm exhausted, but resolve to keep going. We need water and to get out of this place. I relax. My druids are here! They are waiting behind this hut covered by a rocky ridge covered by trees.

Zander has taken some grass away from the back wall of the room and is waving us out.

When I'm close to him, I say, "Head to that ridge, my druids are there. I point with my head.

The dark is complete, but the moon shines enough to see where I indicate. He nods, and our small group hurries to the cover and the men waiting for us. It's Gearoid and all the druids from my forest. Rushing to them reach for them with happy tears.

Gearoid says, "My Phantom Queen, we have been traveling because Sorcha had a vision you needed us. Now that we are here I'm happy we didn't wait or delay. How can we help?"

I answer, "First thing we need food and water. Then I intend to kill every fucking Fomorian in that village. And see if there are any villagers left that we can save."

"I have a plan, goddess if you are so inclined," Sorcha says.

"I can do anything I want. I'm the Mor-Rigan. As long as we don't have to wait I'm in," I agree. All of my men nod, their faces familiar with a stare only warriors understand. We settle in as food and drink is passed to us and listen to the little druid's plan.

26

FINAL BATTLE

*T*he sun is rising. That's our agreed upon signal to move. We have the druids behind us ringing what is left of the village. The chant of their spells fills the air in eerie tones.

I shout, "Turnabout's fair play." I watch as the surprised enemy is frozen in mid-motion.

Tomas and Finn rush forward with swords drawn. They had one giant down and decapitated before the enemy has even figured out we are here.

I take on Croag who was leveling a sword and slash his throat with all my strength. He dies easily. It's a bloody slaughter. I have no remorse. The other men concentrate on the last of the two giants. Zander has hamstrung one, and it is down. The druids chanting is now loud and beats in my chest and my ears. I'm berserker mode now and fight on.

I'm coming out of it when Finn shouts, "Stop Rigan, they are dead! We have killed them all."

I come back to my senses. I'm breathless and move

around the village looking for survivors. The druids found them in a hut close to the one where my group had been held, prisoner. The enemy has tied them hand and foot. Zander and the druids are cutting away the villager's bonds and calming them. Many of the druids have to use the gift I'd given them long ago in the Forest of Rigan. The gift of others believing them is coming in handy so the people here don't fight them.

A young woman with a big belly runs and kneels in front of Rian, the beautiful Fomorian. The boy he had saved it holding onto her skirt. Tears pouring, she says, "I'll be your slave for life, Lord, for saving my son Cathal from the monsters. My name is Deidre."

He gently pulls her to her feet then squats down to Cathal and asks, "You would have escaped without help wouldn't you, big man?"

The little boy is honest, "No sir, I wasn't strong enough. Thank you. I promise I'll get big and strong and help my mama just like you."

Rian replies, "I'm happy I helped you and your Mama." Turning to the lady, "you owe me nothing, but if you remember me and do a kindness to someone else in the future, I'd be eternally grateful."

She answers, "I promise, I will."

I see several cuts on her and move to Rian's side, so she'll notice me. She bows her head, and I stop her with a hand on hers and ask, "Will you let me heal you, daughter?"

"Great goddess Rigan, yes, but there are others who need it more." When we turn to look. The druids have everyone else either taken care of already or being attended to, so she smiles and nods shyly.

Holding her hand, I let the healing flow. Warm and tingling with life the power reaches out. The child within her moves and a vision flashes before my eyes. It's a bother for Cathal, and they will together claim this area as leaders and show the people how-to live-in peace. They will have different roles. Cathal will be the king in this hill country with his brother's support. This child will live long and become one of my druids... his name will be Merlin. I was tired before, but the exhaustion catches up with me and my body trembles and sways with fatigue. Rian is beside me. He holds onto me, and I sink into him for support.

He and the woman walk me over to a stump and seat me. Squatting in front of me he watches me with concern. The girl has sent her son for water. He brought me a cup of honey mead instead and Finn with him.

Finn cuts in-between Rian, and me and looks me over. He blows out his breath and says, "She's exhausted. I'll go make a tent for her and be back to get her. He looks Rian over," Take care of her until I return."

I smile at that, loving he's such a good friend. I glimpse Rian's profile his black curls blowing in the wind and remember that I had seen him in a vision I didn't understand. He is mine. I'm sure. He turns his gaze on me, and his crystal eyes flash. He knows unless I miss my guess.

Sorcha is here now and hands me a new cup and tells me to drink it all it's mistletoe tea and will counteract any lingering poison from the Fomorian cut that had paralyzed me. I don't argue I do what she says. I trust her, then hand the empty cup back. Over her shoulder, I see the pregnant village woman and her brave little son are walking around helping others now and have left Rian and me with Sorcha.

She looks him up and down the same way that Finn

had. I almost laugh, they are so much alike they make a good pair. She says, "Stay here, and I'll bring you some tea."

I have to get this off my chest, so I start, "Rian, I think you know who I am, but you can call me Rigan for now. I have seen visions of you since I was a girl. We are destined for each other. I understand if you wish to avoid this kind of relationship. I want you to know from the beginning before you even have a chance to care. I haven't one but three other lovers. I won't part with them." Before I say more, he hushes me with a finger to my lips.

He begins, "Rigan, goddess, I recognized you at first glance. I have been dreaming of you since I could remember my dreams. You are the only reason I agreed to voyage with the monsters. We can take this slow or as fast as you are comfortable. I will not leave you."

A tear leaks out of my eye thinking of Bran telling me that once. I smile into my Fomorian's crystal eyes, so he knows that I accept him, and this is from happiness and not a rejection. Who would have thought days ago I would love one of the invaders? Not me, but here I am beginning the journey on purpose.

Sorcha is back and hands a cup of tea to Rian. Finn is with her, his hand at her waist. I love they have each other. I'm too tired to bless them or ask Danu right now though and say, "Take me to rest, Rian."

Finn gets the hint, almost no one knows me so well. He guides us to the tent I have been using for this whole war. Before he leaves I ask, "Finn everyone is safe, right?"

His eyes crinkle, and he says, "Yes, goddess. We lost no one, and they are all healed. Rest if we need something I'll come and wake you."

Inside there are nicer blankets and pillows than I'd been traveling with, I guess it's the villager's gift for helping them.

I sink into the pile of blankets and pull Rian with me by his hand. He lays down close to me and we close our eyes knowing we're safe and fall fast asleep.

27

ANOTHER ADDED

*C*omfortable for once, I slept all night. When I wake, I'm alone, and there's a large tub of water waiting for me. I must have been placed magically, or I would have waken up sooner. Dropping my clothes, I sink into the luscious warmth. Someone took care to leave me soap and everything I need to enjoy this bath. I must be scrubbing off a pound of dirt and blood. I have energy to spare when I get out and dress. My hair is going to take me a while to get through, rats' nest is making it sound better than it is. The rustle of the tent cloth is quiet but enough for me to look for who has entered. It's Sorcha with a bottle of something in her hands.

"Great Queen, would you let me brush out your hair? I made a special oil that will help with the tangles," she asks.

"I've always loved my hair brushed Sorcha and yes if you don't mind. I warn you it'll be a challenge," I respond.

I sit and hand her the brush. She takes it and starts on my tangles. I could almost sleep again; it feels so good. But I need to know some things. "Sorcha, I depend on Danu to guide me where Rian is concerned, but I wonder... do you have any misgivings concerning him? Or have you seen or heard anything that would give me a reason to send him on his way and not start a relationship with him?"

"Goddess, I have no misgivings concerning him. The druids in our school have had visions of him for years though. I didn't know until I saw him cover your body to protect you... that it was him. In my visions, he has always appeared as a black panther. I don't know if he *is* a shifter or if that's just his character or spirit animal. I know that he's destined for a place at your side... do you think you should contact the brothers and let them know? Oh, and I'm not saying that you should ask permission, don't get me wrong. You're our great goddess and can decide for yourself what you want without someone telling you what to do. But... if I were you, I wouldn't want to lose any of them if you know what I mean."

The smile on her face is beaming. I return it laughing and say, "You are one-hundred percent correct, druid. Where is Rian, anyway?"

"He's working with the villagers to build back some of their buildings that were torn apart by the fighting."

"That's great and will give me time to contact Mac and Dagda." She's finished with my hair. She worked it into nine double plaits held in the back of my head.

"Your hair is beautiful Mor-Rigan. I'll get out of your way, so you can contact your men and will give you notice if Rian comes this way before you're finished."

"Thank you for understanding. I'll be out as soon as I finish."

As soon as she leaves I get out the rock Dagda gave me and concentrate on him. Seeing him, I wonder why he's such a mess this time of day. He looks as if he's been on a drunken bender.

I say, "Dagda, are you, all right?"

His eyes crinkle, he gives me a goofy and lopsided grin, then slurs, "Rigan, my Queen Consort. I miss you. Please come home." Okay, I'm a little worried.

"That's exactly what I intend to do. I'll start today, but I'm going to the sea first to get Mac. Then, I'll come to the palace. It's going to take me a few days. I'm on the other side of the island, and even if I could fly all the way, it would still be days. Now, tell me what's wrong?"

"Nothing is wrong... well, the witch is bothering me. But she only goes to the dining hall. I have locked her out of my rooms."

"What witch, and why would she be in your rooms?"

At my question, he bursts out laughing. "Are you jealous, love? You have no reason to be. Will you please come home and defend my honor?" And he's laughing again, "I'm serious. Come help me."

"I will. You can count on that. I want to tell you something too. I don't want to tell you in the shape you are in, but you might remember, and it needs to be said. I'll tell you again later. Dagda... Danu has sent me another protector. Nothing has happened between us, but our family is to have another member. Can you possibly accept this?"

"Fuck, Rigan... I don't know. Do you think he'll help me too?"

His brow raises in hope, and I almost laugh at him. "Yes, love I do. I'll be there as fast as I can, and I'll bring help. I love you, handsome."

His words hitch as he says, "I love you too, beautiful. Please hurry."

"I will, I'm on my way."

I stuff my belongings into my pack and head outside where I meet Sorcha who is coming to my direction with Finn right behind her. She hands me some bread with cheese and says, "I get the idea you're ready to leave?"

"I need to talk to Mac, but yes, I have to leave.

Finn nods and says, "I'll get everyone ready."

Finn would you and Sorcha think about staying in this village when we leave. They'll need protection and a druid. You can say no, and I'll ask someone else. I thought...

"Thank you, goddess. We wanted to ask but just didn't know how. It would be our pleasure. We want to be married at Beltane. Would it be possible you could come back to celebrate?"

I walk up to this man who I love like a bother and place a hand on his head and the other on Sorcha's then say, "I bless you and your union. I pray that Danu will bless you as she has me. I'll do my best to be here and I'll miss you terribly." I hug them both before I walk away relieved they will be here for the people and glad they'll be happy.

I take my stone and head to a private area to talk with Mac. When I find a big rock to sit on I do and look into the hole of my stone. Mac appears instantly.

He's tired with bags under his eyes, but he smiles at me. "Rigan, you look beautiful. I'm finished with my work here. The ship is sunk and all the invaders with it. I'll be back soon. I need a couple of hours of sleep before I start. I sense concern, is everything okay?"

"Well, it is now, but it was a test," I tell him everything about this final battle ending with... "now all the Fomorians are dead except the one who protected me, and he's destined to become part of our family. I know it can't be easy to hear this way, but you need to know that the man who saved me will be part of us. His name is Rian."

He sighs, "Rigan, I know you too well to know you are asking permission but that you are asking acceptance. We've talked about him so much that he's been a part of us since childhood. I never thought I would get to be loved by you. I always knew he would. This is not a question for me. I accept him into our relationship."

Whew, that takes a lot off of me, and I relax, but I still have to tell him about Dagda. "That helps, thank you. There's something else. I can't be sure what happened, but I would swear that someone is drugging him and trying to force him into doing something he is refusing to do. My gut says someone is trying for the throne." I continue to tell Mac everything about my earlier conversion with his brother.

He suggests, "Meet me with Rian at the palace. As much as I want to see you first, there's defiantly a problem. I'll try to handle it before you get to Faery. I love you, little bird."

I return, "I love you too." There has been too much loss for me to waste time with wishy-washy feelings. I'm too old for that. They need to know how I feel, and I need to say it. Now I need to tell Bran about Rian, but that can wait. The dead have different opinions about how we live our lives and accept everything as it comes. They want us to include them when it is possible, and I want to tell him in person. I walk back to where my soldiers can see me. We have to leave, and it seems they are all waiting for me. They are wonderful.

Little Cathal is being such a man but has tears streaming down his cheeks when he hugs Rian for the last time. Deidre smiles and holds onto him as we leave. We promise to come back and those faces will make me do it. This village has become one that I'll protect.

I shift and fly with my crows to look over the small group traveling. There isn't any danger. I feel only twinges of worry about what is happening at the Fae Palace and I can't get there soon enough.

When we stop for the night, Tomas and Zander are close enough to their homes that when we leave in the morning, they will split off with their soldiers and return home. We sit around our campfire and tell stories of the journey. We have become close during this campaign. Leaving them will be hard. They too have come under my protection.

The honey mead has me relaxed, and I lay on my blanket dreaming about the good times.

28
PARTING WAYS

In the morning Tomas lingers over his packing so I walk over to him to say my goodbye. "Tomas you have been such a good friend, loyal and strong. I'll miss you. I trust you with the people of the island. You're a good leader and they will flourish with you guiding them. I'll be in my forest some you are always welcome there."

He turns and takes my hands in his rough ones and says, "I don't know what to say. I feel lost. I'll miss you goddess. I'm glad to be out of this fighting but I'm not sure I know how to live a normal life anymore."

I look into the waves of time, silent for seconds. I see him happy with a family and love. Shaking my head and coming back to myself I pull him in for a hug. "You are like a son to me. I've seen your future and I'll seal the path to it for you. I'll tell you a secret. Tomas, the redhead that you think has no use for you, yearns for you. You'll make a family and be happy with her."

He wipes tears from his eyes with the back of his hand and says, "Thank you goddess I needed to know that."

I get my pack ready and pull the flap closed. Zander watches me as he readies himself to mount his horse. He's such a tough one, always trying to take care of others dismissing his own needs. Looking down I check to see if I can glimpse his life lines. I get a glimpse. He takes his time finding a mate but when he does, he's happy and they have a child. I perceive they are happy, and he provides well for them. No hut for him but a rock fortress. Well, I don't have to wonder why he'd build this... extra protection. I need to bless him too, so I walk over to him. The longing in his eyes has me wishing I didn't have to part from him. *He is strong and will be fine.* He isn't like Tomas to reach out a hand, so I do that and take his, he accepts it and holds tight.

I say, "Zander, I'll miss you. I want you to know that any time I'm in my forest you are welcome."

"I will miss you too, goddess, you will always be in my heart." The pain and loneliness I see hurt me. I notice glancing away for a second that Rian is watching us. He's standing by our packs waiting. I calm myself and say, "Zander, you are my trusted leader. I know you'll protect and lead our people the right way. I have looked into the waves of time for you." He is dead silent, so I continue, "when you meet a woman that has a bent pinky finger and dark hair you will find your mate. You will have a child and I have seen that you provide well for them. I bless you and can't wait to see your little one."

He grinds his teeth then says, "Thank you, I love you and will come to the forest to see you." I hug him and hold back the tears so he can hold his. He hops onto his stead and waves goodbye. Both he, Tomas, and the few who stayed with us to the end stop only a few yards away. They turn as one and blow me a kiss before they race off to their homes.

Now I can't hold my tears and I don't mean to sob out loud, but I can't help it. Rian is here and pulls my body into his. He holds me as I let loose the torrent I was holding back. Wiping my face with my hands the best that I can. I look up into his and there are no words. I don't care that my face must be a blotchy mess. I stand on my toes and kiss him softly. His sigh is all I need to hear to know it's all right. He kisses me then and slides his tongue along my lips. Yes, I want him, and I open my mouth. He deepens the kiss and kisses me like I've never been kissed before. He moves back, and I'm not finished so I curl my finger at him to follow me. I find a tree with lots of leaves under it and before I say anything he's taking off his clothes and lays them on the leaves. I take off my shirt but careful not to show anything and turn to put it on top of his. Then looking over my shoulder I smile and tease. He grabs me by the waist and pulls me back into him and bends to nibble on my neck and kiss my shoulders.

I turn not teasing anymore and he sucks in his breath, "You are gorgeous, Rigan. I want to share something with you, is that all right?"

I nod yes and wait. He puts a finger to my forehead and blows lightly on it. Then says in my head, *"I want to speak with you this way, and share how I feel so you can feel my passion for you."*

"Ah, that's intense! I'm glad. I love this, thank you."

I feel his need and he's burning with it, It burns me back. He takes off his shoes then pants, I'm not waiting and take off mine. Our bodies crash together, his kisses ignite my fire and I'm ready. He's so tender, but strong and inserts a finger inside of me making sure I'm ready... slowly he enters me. Oh, he's very large and stretches me to the limit. He waits and lifts my ass closer to him with little pressure. I want him all now but he's taking this slow because of his size. I push him up to see his face better and he sinks into me deeper. I can't stand it and reach for my nipples to turn him on. *Ah, so he feels what I feel too!* His breathing is faster, and he pushes in more. "Rian, I'm going to come."

He bobs his head and says, "Rigan, come on me and when you do, I'll fuck you and make you come again."

Holy shit! To hear him say it is enough and I throb an orgasm to beat all orgasms. He goes balls deep into me and leans forward on his arms holding me. I thrust into him to help him. Our rhythm is perfect until I throb and tingle coming again, he groans, "I'm coming, beautiful."

I love the weight of him on top of me, but I know he's tired and I push him a little. He flips onto his back leaving his arm around me. I let him sleep for a time and smile when I see the leaves in his hair the same as the pool had shown me long ago. I watch the waves of time again. They show me precious little, but I can see the witch that's trying to get my other man. Yeah, that isn't happening! We'll be there soon.

Rian wakes in a short while and we dress talking the whole time. I tell him what has happened when I told Mac and Dagda about him. He says, "So they both accept me?"

"Yes, and we'll be great together. I want us all together, but If you don't want to live in the palace or in Faery, you can live in my forest. I'll leave that up to you, but we need to go to the palace first and save Dagda from whatever it is the witch has planned."

"Yes, I agree. We'll travel faster if we shift. I don't want to scare you, but I am a panther. Can you handle it if I shift in front of you?"

"I can, you know I'm a shifter already. I'll shift into my wolf so we can run together. The sooner we get there the better. Mac will meet us there." He nods his ascent, and we put on our packs to shift. It's magic and whatever I have on shifts with me I see that it's the same with him. Good lord, he's gorgeous. His panther gleams in the sunshine his muscles move with every breath. Not waiting we both head into our destiny.

29

IT WAS WORTH IT

*L*eaves crunch under our paws, it isn't a loud noise. We stop outside the village of Torn where this journey started. I watch the villagers go about their day. It makes me feel the battle was worth it. As a crow, I sit on Rian's panther shoulders and watch the children play. Eva has the baby out on a blanket in the sunshine while her brothers jump and play like faeries around her. Their giggles make me happy.

Eimer comes up without a sound and pulls me out of my thoughts when she asks, "My lady, is there trouble? Can I help? Shall I warn the people?"

I shift to talk to her. "No, lovely girl. I just wanted to watch the children play. The battles have been hard, and it's nice to see them safe and sound. How is everything here? Everyone healthy?"

"Yes, as long as we can keep the brownies from too many tricks there's nothing to worry about here," she laughs then says, "thank you for that great queen. We have a wonderful life."

That brings a tear to my eyes. I say, "Not all me, but thank you for knowing that I have a part in your protection. I'd like you to meet Rian.

Ever the gentleman he shifts and does a little bow taking her hand and kissing the air above it. She blushes. *Oh, girl, I do understand.*

"We are on our way to Faery to meet with Manannan Mac Lir and King Dagda. Have you seen either of them?" I'm ready to be on my way now that I have said their names.

"No, but I can tell you, goddess, the forest is unsettled. There's something different I can't pin down. I know you'll understand when you enter though. Maybe it's lonely and misses you being home. Will you let me make you some tea? Come over here and hold the baby."

"Oh yes, that will make me stay for a little longer. When I walk over Eva picks up the little one and hands her to me saying, "Rigan, look how she's grown, and she's the best little thing. Aed, will you get the goddess a pillow to sit on?"

The handsome boy shoots off with a smile and is back before I have time to think. I'm all wrapped up in the baby and making faces at her as she coos. Aed, her older brother, looks so happy plumping the pillow for me I smile and sit for him accepting what he's so considerately done for me. Eva smiles at that too especially when he climbs into Rian's lap when he sits beside me. My heart is overflowing with joy. It was worth every scratch! This is what I want for my people. I can live with myself now knowing that this is the outcome of so much bloodshed. Even if it started out to be just to get revenge for Bran, it became so much more.

The baby is squirming, and I know she's hungry turning her face to my breast. I have a moment of want, wondering if I'll ever give birth to a child of my own. The Tuatha de do not easily get pregnant; that's why so many human children are taken and raised by faeries. Eva takes the little one and lowers her top to nurse her. A vision starts, and I see... Eva is already carrying her next child another son. He will be special like the baby girl, and they will be close. Then clouds cover my vision, and I can't see more.

Eimer hands me a cup of tea, and I relax. I can't remember the last time I was stress-free. It might make me sad if I did. It's late enough that the men of the village are coming home from the fields. Liran, Eva's husband, sees me and rushes over. We stand, and he says, "No relax goddess and you too, young man." I have to smile at that. Fomorians are long lived, Rian is probably twice Liran's age. *Hmm... I need to ask him.* I might just have robbed the cradle. It doesn't matter though we're made for each other. Liran continues, "I have a big fat boar in the pit that has been roasting for a day. Please let us honor you goddess and give thanks for all you do for us?"

"Let's stay tonight, Rian. I think it'll be okay. Mac isn't in Faery yet or he would have sent word. Rejecting the gift will only shame them. I'd rather accept and honor them. Dagda's strong, and I don't feel that his life is in danger."

He responds, *"I think we're close enough love that we could get there quickly if he needs us. And you're right about Mac, he might find us here easier than Faery."*

"Liran, this is Rian, my consort. We would love to share a meal with you. I hear your roasted pig is the best in the whole island," I say.

The village leader smiles and lifts his shoulders then says, "Good then let's make the goddess feel at home everyone. Then without an ounce of magic, the day feels charmed as we're fed and blessed with every dessert they could find.

The whole village gathered around in the center of the town. A large fire pit is lit, and a group of teenagers dance for us. They are beautiful and so skilled that the dance amazes me. Everyone is quiet and still now that the dance is over. *How will I repay this blessing? I know, I'll tell them a story.* I get up and walk around the circle, and a hush falls.

I say, "My lovely people you have blessed us tonight and to thank you I'll tell you a story. Is that something you might like?" That's like asking if they like honey mead. They shout and laugh that I should start before they beg me for a long story.

I sit on a rock ledge built up for the storytellers next to the fire pit. "I must tell you ahead of time, this story is true. You might think it's just made up for your entertainment, but no, it's real, and the ones involved are too. They live far from here and in another time. It will still be a good lesson for you. This story starts at Samhain when a lord of a rich king in a far country fell to sleep and dreamed of the most beautiful woman he'd ever seen. Of course, she was one of the ladies of our fair island. The young lord fell in love with her in his dreams. He woke in the middle of the night wanted her with every cell in his body. A spirit roaming passed by his window and saw him and wondered why he was so upset so stopped to speak with him. You know the dead walk at Samhain even in other countries even if they don't notice them. The young lord saw this ghost and told him that he would die of need because his love is only in his dreams. But when the man described the girl, the spirit knew that he was dreaming of the goddess of dreams, one of our very own fair ladies. He told him I know where your lady lives, and she is real, but you will be tested to have her." I look around at the rapt faces and make it even more real, so

I ask, "Have any of you been spoken to by a loved one or another on Samhain?"

Liran answers, "No, goddess we stay inside and hide from the spirits who roam on that night!" Everyone laughs including me.

I continue, "Well the young lord was not afraid and did as the spirit told him. He must travel taking with him a gift of his most priceless riches to offer her when they meet. He starts out with a big chest of treasure. On the way, thieves accosted him and lost all of his treasure. He had nothing but the dreams that came every time he slept. That kept him moving toward his love. The young man was very handsome. His hair cut in the latest fashion, and his clothes made of the finest cloth, his love would still want him he thought. As he traveled he was robbed again, this time of his beautiful clothes were taken, he was beaten and left to die. Dirty and with nothing he kept going until he came to a calm blue stream and stopped to get a drink of water. Seeing his reflection in the water he cried. His love will never want him now. He has no good looks anymore. In fact, he has nothing and lost everything just searching for her. He washes in the water to at least be clean when he finds her. When he dresses in the rags, the robbers had left him he spots a bush full of the ripest most beautiful blackberries. Not having eaten in a while he takes them and fills up then takes a cloth and picks more for his meal later then starts out on his quest again. In just a few miles down the path, he meets an old hag who greets him.

He answers her saying, "Good day to you old mother. How is your day?"

She croaks, "I'm tired and hungry. Will you help me?"

It's getting dark, and the young man knows it isn't safe, so he finds the old woman a sheltered spot under a large tree and makes a little fire to keep her warm. He gives her all of his berries. She takes them and doesn't even share. Then they fall asleep on the thick bed of leaves under the tree. He dreams, and his love tells him to awake she has gotten his gift and she wants to be with the man who would give her such a fine thing. He is surprised and tells her he's lost her gift. She insisted that she got it and wants him to wake up. He opens his eyes, and instead of the hag, he sees his love. He cries because he has nothing for her.

She says, "My love, my life, you have kept traveling to find me even when robbed and beaten. You were kind to the old hag who I was pretending to be and gave me all of your berries. Your unselfishness to a stranger is the best gift I could ever desire. He takes her in his arms, and she kisses him, and his clothes are magically changed back to the ones he had before, and the chest of treasure is at his feet. He laughs and picks her high in the air swinging her around in his happiness. Looking around the circle again I ask, "Does anyone here know the moral of this story?"

No one speaks. Then Rian says with his deep quiet voice, "Always take care of strangers. They might not be who they appear."

I say, "Just so."

Then thinking of having some fun... I shift into my hag Morrigan and swoop over to the nearest of the teen dancers and getting in her face say, "BOO!"

She screams, grabs hold, and pulls me in for a hug. Everyone is laughing again, and we stay up late letting more people tell their stories before retiring. Liran has put us up in a guest hut, and we gladly go in to sleep with happy hearts.

30

CUTE TWINS

*W*hen Rian and I get to the rock wall leading into the Fae Realm I look around to be sure no one is here to see us, then raise my arms to bring on a mist to cover us even more. A hand holds onto my arm. I jerk around thinking of attacking and seeing that it's my Mac and jump into his arms.

"I'm so happy to see you, Mac! You are pretty sneaky coming up without me hearing."

"Oh, my little crow, I've missed you!" He kisses me long and hard. We stop when we hear Rian clear his throat. "Maybe I should let you continue but know that I'm here and enjoying the show."

"Mac, this is Rian," I say.

Mac, looks at the ground as he swaggers over to Rian. I hold my breath wondering what's going to happen. Then Mac holds out his hand to Rian and shakes it. He says, "Welcome Rian, I think we shall be good friends and more one day. Thank you for saving Rigan. I heard that you put yourself in danger to protect her. I can't thank you enough.

Make a pact with me that one of us will always be with her."

A brilliant smile bursts over Rian's features and he answers, "It's a deal. Shall we add Dagda to this pact?"

He motions toward the opening, and we all move forward. I pull a thick mist back up to cover us from prying eyes. Then Rian bounces back like he's run into a wall and almost loses his feet. Mac puts his hands out and feels something. I move and do the same, it's a barrier. I glance over to the men.

"What is this and who would do this?" I wonder.

We turn as one when a soft voice behind us says, "It's a barrier to keep you out Mor-Rigan. I saw Medb, and her brownies put it here after you left for war."

Standing before us is a wood nymph. I remember seeing her before. She is an amazing beauty. Red locks that hang past her waist, green eyes that border on blue, and a body men would kill for and probably have. She looks back at me with an embarrassed stare. It isn't easy for a wood nymph to speak to anyone. This is brave for her to even be a few steps away from her tree. I notice she has several faeries buzzing around her, they must be her people.

I walk toward her slowly to put her at ease and say, "Child of the Forest of Rigan, I'm in your debt. Do you know more? Would you share it with us? You may call me Rigan, this is Manannan Mac Lir, and Rian.

She smiles shyly at me and returns, "I'm Elora, Your Majesty. You owe me nothing you and your forest provides for my friends and me. I know your consorts too. I do know a little more. Will you come to my tree? I can tell you what I know; it's a strain to be so far away from him." I know she is referring to her tree as he and am not surpised.

Rian says in my thoughts, *"I'll walk behind you and guard."*

"Okay, but I'm sure it's all right."

I reach for Mac's hand, and we follow Elora to her tree. Hidden in the side is an opening which we enter then walk down several steps into a wonderland apartment. Everything here is earthy. Chairs made of wood tied with vines topped with soft orange pillows. The rugs look like flowers but are tough enough to walk upon. The tree nymph takes Mac's other hand and seats him, then me, then points to a chair for Rian. She says, "I'll be right back."

I nod to her. When she's gone, I look up and see there's a light way up high in the top of the tree, it's reflected off of various mirrors which light up the room. I love it here, no wonder she hates to leave. I turn to the guys, and they are also in wonderment at our surroundings. Elora comes back into the room with a tray of cups and a picture of something and pours us all a cup. It's faery brandy. I drink all of mine, it's the best I've ever tasted.

She pours me more and begins, "Rigan, goddess, while you have been gone. Medb has made a play for the Faery throne. You know her, don't you?"

My soul goes cold. "I've heard of her, but don't know her. She's the goddess of Intoxication. What has she done? Is Dagda all right, do you know?"

"As far as I know he's locked himself in his room and refuses to leave. He has little faeries that bring him food, water, and information. That's how I know what is happening. The drunken goddess thinks she has sealed the realm away from the Earth realm so that you can't enter, but we know other ways."

"I know you can't leave your tree for long. Will you send

one of your friends to show us the way, Elora? Is there anything else I need to know?"

"You are such a smart goddess, always asking the right questions. Yes, you need to know that just stepping into the palace will render you drunk. She has spelled the entire castle and surrounding grounds. I just gave you the antidote in your brandy to protect you. I'll give you more, it doesn't last and will wear off." She takes a little purple faery off of her shoulder and hands him to me with another who is in blue. "These are my friends please be good to them. Their names are Perf and Kerf, they are twins. They can show you the way and are very brave."

"I'll take the best of care with you two. Nice to meet you," I say.

The faeries bow and say together, "Follow us, fair queen." And they zip away. I can't even guess where they are. They return and fall over themselves then with hands on their hips ask, "Are you coming?"

I smile, "Most definitely, but can you move slow enough I can keep up? Please?"

They put their hands over their mouths and giggle, "Yes, slow one, we can." They move to the door and wait for us. We give thanks to Elora and say goodbye. She shoves a skin of brandy into Mac's hands as we leave. I think she must like him. I get the sentiment.

THE TWIN FAERIES take us to a circle of stones and stop. So, we pause as well. They just look at me.

"I feel I'm missing something here guys. Can you help a girl out?"

They fall on the ground laughing. *Okay, this will be fun.*

"I'll help, beautiful," Rian says.

Rian says to the hysterical twins, "So guys, I get the idea that you have brought us to a gate. Is this new magic?"

It sobers them right up. You can tell they are proud of the circle magic so begin to explain. Perf says, "Yes, great Fomorian shifter. The faeries of the forest have pooled their magic and made faery circles. If you enter the faery circle with one of us, you will go through the barrier between the realms and into Faery where the Tuatha de live."

Rian says, "That is amazing magic. We are with you will you show us the way now?"

They wave their tiny hands for us to step into the ring. We do without hesitation. Then with sly grins, they enter with us and swoosh the lights flare, and we're literally sucked into Faery. The twins immediately hide and while I try to keep my feet without getting sick.

They say together, "There's the king's palace. We'll stay will you and keep you out of trouble."

I almost giggle but hold it, my stomach still rolling makes it easy.

Mac says, "My cloak is large enough to fit us all if we're close together. Get under with me, and we can walk to the doors. As soon as someone opens them go in."

We all squeeze together. I put my arm around him and Rian. He covers us, and we move toward the back entry to the palace kitchen. The doors open and hands appear and throw out dirt from a dustpan. It's Flora. I wonder what she's doing here. I thought Dagda banished her and her lover. We step in just after she turns to go back into the kichen.

31

WE CAN DO THIS

 ac, Rian, the twins, and I stand frozen in the palace kitchen. Flora sets the dustpan in the corner and almost tips over. She sits by the fire where Tirn, her fiancé, is already sitting. They are talking so we listen to the errant couple.

Flora says, "Tirn, I just saw the funniest thing. I think the Phantom Queen is here!" She screeches in glee, she disappeared before I was sure. Won't it be funny to see her and Madb fight it out? That old witch couldn't hold a candle to the Queen Consort."

Flora gets up and sways on her feet obviously drunk. Tirn catches her around the waist laughing. He puts a finger to his lips and says, "Shh, we should go find her and tell her we're sorry and offer our help. That way we can pay her back for doing her wrong. We were so wrong, my love." He sniffs and starts crying.

Just watching them makes me feel a little drunk myself. I need a drink of the brandy. I motion for Mac to take off the cloak, so the couple can see us. When he takes it off, and the drunk couple can see us their eyes go wide. Flora shuffles over as fast as she can and pushes me into the herb closet. With absolutely no grace she waves the others in before closing the door. The twins are watching from Mac's shoulders. I can't help but think of them as good and evil and smile wondering which is which. It smells like cinnamon in here. The closet is a large room with all kinds of herbs and vegetables even some apples all neatly put away in baskets on shelves. There is even some art in here… that makes no sense.

Before Flora says a word, I say, "Give me a drink of the brandy please Mac, I'm getting drunk just being close to these two. When we have all had a sip, my mind is clearer. I continue, "Flora, where is the intoxication goddess and where the hell is Dagda?"

She is coming around and shakes her head before she answers. Tirn puts his hand on her back at her waist to give her support and encourage her.

"My Phantom Queen, I'm so sorry. I was stupid. We…"

"Apology accepted, now you can make it up to me and tell me where my king is!"

"Your Highness, he's locked in his room, and no one can get in. He sealed his door with a magic spell and even if it didn't repeal anyone trying to open it, it's impossible to open without a key. We have been too drunk to think straight, but now I'm sober I remember something about it, there was a secret tunnel to your room from this closet. I haven't used it or seen it but was told by the chef."

"Start looking everyone," I say and run my hand along the walls. There *is* a difference in the end wall. Mac and Rian help me move the shelf that's there out of the way. We are all running our hands over the wall… and nothing. I have an idea and walk over to the artwork and look behind it. Yes! There's an impression with a handle. I pull it out and turn the handle and the wall opens with a scraping sound.

"I'm going in. Flora, will you please close this door and stay close to the kitchen, so I can find you?"

"I can do that. I won't let you down again, Queen Consort," She affirms.

Tirn stays with his lady. Mac and Rian follow me without question. I wait to be sure the wall is closed, and no one is following. It is dark as pitch. Perf and Kerf make a light for us with their bodies like little lightning bugs but better. I move ahead there's only one way to go, then a set of stairs. After the stairs is a door.

"Be ready for anything," I whisper.

The men nod, and I move to touch the doorknob Rian pulls me back into him, and Mac squeezes his big ass in front of me. With a little pressure Rian pushes me forward into Mac. I reach around him automatically. His abs are always sexy, and this is a great place to be. I turn as much as possible to see Rian and his big shit-eating grin. I grin back. Then Mac has the door open, and that moment is gone. I sniff and sneeze from the dust in the room mixed with... my own perfume. We are in my chambers. I move to the door that connects with Dagda's, and it opens. His surprised face is flushed red. He rushes to me and scoops me up. Rian has the door closed behind us and is locking it.

I'm crying and giggling at the same time. Dagda is happy but still swaying on his feet and loses his balance trips across the room, almost gets his balance, runs into the table, spins, and we flop onto the bed.

"Great aim you got there, Faery King," I chuckle.

"I could have a greater... hiccup... aim if these two will

just leaves sush alone... hiccup... for an hour or two," he slurs doing better than I thought he could. The witches spell must be doubled for him.

Mac and Rian smile at each other, they're enjoying this, unless I miss my guess.

"Just hand me the brandy guys," I demand.

I hand the skin to Dagda, he takes a deep draught then looks at us and bellows a great laugh. "I'm so glad you're here and made it into our rooms, my love. I'm not sure I would have opened the door. They have tried to fake your voice many times already." With that, he stands lifting me with him and standing with his arm around me. Taking a deep emotional breath, he walks up to Mac and gives him a big hug patting him on the back. When he backs up, he says, "Brother, I've missed you almost as much as our great queen. And who are these little faeries?" he asks pointing to Perf and Kerf.

Mac answers, "They are friends who showed us the way here since the way to the realm has been shut. They are friends from the Forest of Rigan and stayed with us when we arrived. They will help us if they are able."

The king shakes their hands, and they do the most formal faery bows.

Dagda then turns to Rian, "You must be our new Fomorian. You're welcome here," he says and holds his hand out to shake. Rian takes his hand and clasps it with his other.

Rian says, "Thank you. Now, we need to know what has happened that you would be locked in your room and the rest of the people intoxicated so we can plan a return to normalcy."

"I'm not sure I remember everything correctly. I have been in here for a while. I have water, but I have had to conjure food or depend on faeries to bring it. The drunken-ness never went away until you gave me the brandy. I don't know where to start."

Mac says, "Start anywhere Dagda. We'll keep up. We have been strategizing for months, and it's become second nature. Anyway, if you don't our little crow will go out on her own to defend you, and we don't want that. She licks blood from her blade and shit like that, just to make a point! It's all pretty gory."

"I'll do my best in that case. When you left, Rigan, I got depressed, and some court members saw that it was progressing the longer you were gone. It became harder to suppress the trouble makers who I believed were trying to hurt you, my love. The court made me feel better by having a celebration party and invited the intoxication goddess to make it more fun. She's a party animal, and those who wished to replace you thought she was a great option. Tornitch had overheard a conversation between her and Zarg one of my top councilmen. They were plotting to over-throw me and take the throne while you were away. It later came to light at the party that they were working with the Fomorians to ensure they killed you in battle. When I heard that... I might have gone a bit crazy and tried to kill her. That's when everything went drunk, I mean very drunk. They were shouting at me to sign over the government and make a vow they were the rulers of the Tuatha De. At first, it was all I could do to understand them and Zarg made Madb ease up her spell on me. When she did, I ran here and locked myself in. They have been trying every threat in the book to get me to hand over the kingdom. They even said you had all been killed in the war. If you hadn't contacted me, I would have believed them. You know that witch has a dog by her side at all times? She calls him Moddey Dhoo, he's anything but cute. I think he's part wolf and part demon. That's all I can think of for now. I'll tell you if I think of something I've forgotten."

I say, "I think we have enough to work with, handsome. Let's move over to the desk so I can write some things down. First things first, what other magic does Madb have that she can use against us and what is Zarg's magic? Do they have others helping them and who will help us?"

My handsome king grins and gives us all the information we need to plan our re-taking of the palace from the wicked bitch of the west. We all have a part and hope we don't have to rely on Plan B and fly by the seat of our pants.

I send the twins to get Flora and Tirn. Mac goes to see if he can find Tornitch and any others loyal to the king... we will need them all.

32

TAKING THE WITCH DOWN

*O*ur group of warriors sits around the room. Tirn had gotten his friends from the stables to help, and Tornitch had gotten several of the trusted council members in on the plan.

I pace and ask, "Is everyone sure what your part in the takeover is and are you positive you can carry it out? If you can't there's no shame, just let me know."

All our cohorts quietly respond, "Yes."

"Then let's begin. Thank you all, I pray Danu's favor on us all. Council members and Tornitch leave first and be careful. We'll see you in the dining hall when the food is served."

All of our help filters out through the secret passage and into the kitchen. My men and I are left alone for the first time in hours. I'm already thinking of little surprises for each of them. *Wow, can I get my mind out of the gutter for once?* Even as wound up as I am, looking forward to being with them is in the front of my thoughts. I wish I could relax with them but until this is over it would be a mistake.

Rian knows my thoughts now that I've accepted his

magic, so we could speak to each other telepathically. He moves close putting his hands on my waist but looking at Mac and Dagda. Grinning like a demon the king moves forward to my left and Mac grits his teeth and moves to my left.

Rian says, "Rigan, we don't have time for what we really want to show you but just a small taste before we go. A way to remember what we're fighting for... if you are up for it. I guarantee we are."

"I...," I almost said I don't know then Rian lowers his mouth to my neck and bites me. What really happens is, I groan because it feels so good. That's enough for the other two.

Dagda crushes his lips to mine and says, "I've missed you so much, Rigan. I can't wait to have more time with you. I want to see you naked." I growl into his mouth.

Mac has put his hand in my top and is rubbing slow circles teasing my nipples getting one with his fingers and the other with his wrist... it's making me weak. I'm forgetting what we are about to do.

Dagda moves and lets Mac kiss me, and he takes his time before allowing Rian have my mouth. I'm squirming and can't help but rub myself on his leg. Mac lifts my hair and is kissing me from the back now. I can feel his hard dick press into my ass. Dagda reaches to my wet slit, and I almost jump out of my skin; it feels so wonderful. I can't be quiet. The moans are getting louder, and Rian covers my entire mouth to hush me. I'm not holding back; this is too hot. I stiffen and shatter on Dagda's hand. I want more but know that this is it when they loosen their hold on me.

The fire in their eyes isn't making this any easier, but I say, "I can't wait for the rest. Right now, let me try to concentrate. I'm not sure I can." After a pause I continue, "Do all of you have your weapons?"

We do a check then we go stand by the door and Dagda opens it. We peek out, and there are two guards on the ground tied up and out for the count. Thank you, Tirn and the stable boys. We make our way down the hall to the dining room and find the guards there are trussed up like the others. I nod to Dagda, and he enters first with us behind him. He swings his club back and forth across every foe who tries to get close taking them out in one blow.

The first thing I look for is if Perf and Kerf got that demon dog drugged and out of the hall. The answer is no. They are off to the side of the front table. With a pork chop in their hands hanging on for dear life and fighting the dog for it. Plan B for this idea. I wave at the cauldron, core ansic, and bring it down on them all. I'll have to make sure the twins survived first chance.

But first... the bitch. Dagda is going straight for Zarg. That is his assigned task, and he's staying with the plan which makes it easy for me to hunt down Madb. I find her quickly. The bitch is raising her hands to start a spell. I morph into my crow, fly full speed, and stab her in the eye with my beak. When she tries to pry me loose, I change to my wolf. She's fighting back but isn't the fighter I am. With her throat between my teeth, I'm about to chomp it in half when she begs for her life.

I'll give that decision to Dagda. It will prove his power and that he is king here, so I wait. The room has gone quiet except for my growls. Dagda says, "Madb swear fealty and that you will never come against this kingdom again. In fact, any in this room."

She begs, "I swear it! Please, get her off of me and let me

live. I promise! You will have my loyalty and peace, you and everyone here. You are king of the Tuatha de Danann."

I wait for my handsome king. He motions with his head, so I let her go and transform into my human shape, my hand to her throat I slam her against the wall.

I warn, "If I ever see you again I'll kill you. Leave now! Don't wait."

She leaves and takes her minions with her. I go to stand by my men who have fought all the enemy in the room. Zarg was not as lucky as Madb and lays dead on the floor with his head crushed. Everyone else is okay.

I roll my eyes and go to lift the cauldron and make sure the twins survived. When I raise the pot, those crazy faeries are leaning on the dog with happy smiles. He has grease splotched all over and is busy licking it off. Whatever I'm glad they are alive, and everyone is laughing.

Mac speaks, "If there are any here who would contest Dagda's right to reign I will fight you in fair combat here and now.

Rian says, "I'm with him."

The room stays silent until one of the loyal council members claps. The place breaks out in applause, and several move forward and congratulate the king.

Dagda looks to Tornitch, he grins with only his eyes, and with a wave of his hand, a troop of faeries has the room cleaned by magic in an instant. Then the chefs bring in food for a real feast, and we dine and drink but are careful not to get drunk as the realm celebrates with us. Now, if I can just get to a tub and these men alone again.

33

I DID SOMETHINGS RIGHT

*I*t has been a few weeks since our battle with Madb. Things are different now that the kingdom is settled. Dagda has appointed Mac his emissary to the sea and Rian an Ambassador for the entire island and Faery. I've wanted to go the Otherworld and talk to Bran. There isn't a reason to wait and won't put it off any longer. I need to see him; he doesn't know about Rian, and I want him to know. I don't like feeling that I'm sneaking around on him.

It's a little dark in the hallway on my way to meet my men in the king's throne room. With a wave of my hand, I paint the walls a crisp pale cream color. Oh, I like that so much better than the cold gray stone. When I get to the doorway, I see Dagda, Mac, and Rian talking and making plans for a vacation. I like that idea. But first Bran...

I say, "I'm ready to leave. I'll be back soon. Bran can't stay will me long to talk, but I'll stay with him as long as he's able. Rian is closet to me and reaches to pull me close and asks, "Should I go with you, beautiful?"

"No, this is a safe trip, and I'm used to the Otherworld. If

I'm not home tonight for dinner, then come with your swords swinging. Anyway, you can tell what I'm thinking, I'll scream," smiling I touch his face and kiss him lightly.

I move to Mac who is waiting. He pulls me close putting one hand just under my breast closer to the front of my body. I relish the feel, now that's sexy. When I see his serious look, I say, "You of all people know I'll be safe on this trip. I'll be home as soon as Bran has to return through the gates."

"Okay, but if you aren't here tonight, I'll be coming for you with the others for war. I'm not putting up with anything happening to you." I smile and kiss him again and pull away. He purposefully flicks a finger up and across my nipple giving me a shiver. I raise my brow and give him a flirty look.

When I get to Dagda, he is grinning like a fool. Yes, I can tell he saw, but no they can't detain me this way even though I'm thinking about it. I play coy. "Dagda, keep Mac and Rian warm for me. I want to swim in the garden with you three after I get home. Does that sound fun?"

"What sounds fun is what happens when we're in the pool." He bends his head, and the kiss is one that makes me want more. I pull back before I can't stop and have no control. Rolling my eyes at him, I say, "Almost worked, but I'm going."

"Be safe, love. I know you can take care of yourself. I'll be waiting for you."

I leave them in the throne room planning and walk to the kitchens. The whole way I'm humming to myself and painting the walls. The kitchen is warm, and I find Artis eating a piece of an oatcake. He's not looking quite as skinny as he did before. He smiles at me and asks, "My lady, would you like to walk with me into the forest?"

"I need to be somewhere Artis, but I'll go with you for a

short walk, then I must leave. I have a date," I say looking to the others in the kitchen. My stomach growls and the chef, Joey hands me an oak cake with honey of my own. I sit when Flora brings me a stool, I sit and eat. I notice that Perf and Kerf are flirting around her. I wonder why they didn't go back to the forest and the wood nymph, Elora.

I say, "Thank you, Joey, the food is delicious. I was in a hurry and not thinking. And thank you for the stool, Flora. By any chance are you expecting?"

Her smile is beaming, "Yes goddess, but it's very new. I haven't told Tirn even yet."

"I'll keep it to myself. Congratulations and Danu bless you." I wipe my fingers on a towel sitting on the table and get up to give her a hug. Now, I need to get going. Hand in hand Artis and I skip down the path and go straight to the pool.

I ask, "Artis, does someone ask you to bring me to the pool?"

He looks at the ground, grinding his toes into the dirt. I won't press him. I pat him on the shoulder, so he knows it's okay not to answer. Then look into the pool. I assume there's something I need to see or understand. The pool is still dark. I move closer and what looks like the bottom of the water is land, and it's different from what I'm used to seeing. It's farmland and not so full of trees. I know it is my island of the future. Many pictures hold my interest then the face of a woman. She surprises me and speaks in my thoughts. "Mor-Rigan, daughter of Tuatha de Danann. I want to show you something you have done."

I say, "Yes, I'm here, my lady of the water. I'll watch." Inside my soul is quaking. I feel sick. I've done so much bad. Is this a punishment for all my wrongdoing? I'll watch and take my punishment if that's what this is and learn from it.

The lady turns grandly with her arm stretched out to show me where to look. When I do, I see... Eva and Liran happy and their family playing together in a spring. "They would not have this if you hadn't given of yourself and helped the woman at the baby's birth." *One good thing.*

Now there is a picture of Zander and Tomas at the battle we stopped over the stealing of brides, and the image moves on to show them at home with happy families. "These would be dead if you had not helped and stopped the battle. The children of these men will make the country strong."

Then I see one of the Fomorians who I had taken to the Otherworld helping the army of the dead. He's smiling. "He would be a wondering fetch in pain in this world if you hadn't helped him move on. A slave to the Fomorians and yet he served with respect. He and his mother deserved the honor of a decent afterlife." That surprises me, tears slide down my face, I might have done something right. As if answering my thought, she says, "You have done lots of good for others, daughter. I could stay all day and show you things you have discounted. Yes, I know you aren't perfect, but you aren't evil either. You have made it a purpose to help and protect others on our island, and there is this..."

I see Rian in his homeland people are bowing to him and calling him brother, he is loved. His crystal blue eyes beam and shine. Then the monsters take him on a ship and even though he's not treated well, he behaves well in every instance. Then I see when he covered me with his body. My torque had fallen off my neck, and he had just enough life to put it back on me. Then he's still and appears to die. I never knew.

"It seems as if he's the one who you were promised to, doesn't it, Rigan?"

Confused I say, "Yes, but lady, what does this mean?"

A voice behind me says, "It means... "I turn and, in the place, where Aris had been is the Earth mother, Danu. Radiant light pouring from her I start to bow, and she stops me with and hand to mine and a small shake of her head. My body is shaking with hope as I listen to her next words.

It means that the warrior, Rian, died on the field that day protecting you. I gifted you by placing the soul of your beloved Bran in him as his heart stopped. I revived him and clouded his memory with Rian's, until this moment he has believed he is the warrior Rian. But no more, I have returned his memory this minute as a reward to you for doing good for me. Don't worry about the warrior his spirit is with me in the heavens. He will be reborn as a king. In fact, the unborn Merlin, brother to Aed, who lives in the village of the last battle, will be his friend and helper.

I'm crying so hard I can't speak, but I try and make no sense. She raises her hand and blows a kiss. I calm, blink, and wipe the tears off my face. When I look back up, she is gone.

I hoot in glee swirling in a circle and say, "Thank you, Earth mother! I love you!"

"I love you too." I hear the whisper on the wind.

I shift into my crow and fly as fast as I can back to the palace to start my new life with the loves I can't live without. This will be a wonderful life!

The End

Glossary

This isn't an all-inclusive list but some so that you have an idea of some of the pronunciations for the some of the character's names and a few other things.

Badb – (Bibe or Bahdb the last b being almost a th or v but softer) Rigan's sister and Bean Sidhe.

Bean Sidhe's – (Banshee) Badb, who heralds the death of family members by shrieking a call.

Cathal – (Ka hal) The little boy that Rian saved from the giant.

Cian – (Kee-an) Druid under Gearoid from the Forest of Rigan.

Coire ansic – (Kwera ahn sik) - the cauldron that never runs dry.

Dagda – (Dag Da or Da Da) King of the Tuatha de Danann.

Danu – (Dan oo) The mother goddess.

Dierdre – (Deer drah) Mother of Cathal.

Enbarr – (In Bahr) Mac's black horse.

Ernmas – (Ur-mas) Rigan's mother.

Fachan – (Fachin) A monster with one eye and one arm that comes from its chest.

Fetch – (Fech) An unhappy soul roaming and haunting and trying to inhabit the living. They double as someone who just died or is alive to fool the people usually for their own purposes.

Finn – (Fin) One of Rigan's warrior crows.

Fomorians – (Foe more e an) The invading enemy, monsters, goblins, and ice giants. There are also humans in this group.

Forest of Rigan – The forest where Rigan lives and where her following druids find her.

Fragrach – (Fra ger rach) Mac's sword.

Gearoid – (Gar ret) The leader of the druids who follow Rigan

Lorg mór – (Lorg more) Dagda's club, it kills nine at once with one end or gives life with the other.

Madb – (Mab) The goddess of Intoxication.

Macha – (Ma ka) Rigan's motherly sister who collects heads on the battlefield.

Manannan Mac Lir – (Ma nan an mac leer) One of the gods of the sea and Rigan's best friend.

Otherworld – The place past the veil of death where Rigan

takes the souls of those who die. There are separate places in this realm.

Rian – (Ree on) A Fomorian who saved a boy from the giants.

Rigan - (Ree-gan) The Mor-Rigan, The Phantom Queen.

Samhain – (Sow in) A holiday we call Halloween.

Sorcha – (Sor cha) Auburn haired druid from the Forest of Rigan.

Tomas – (Toe mas) A chieftain of a tribe of people on the island.

Tornitch – (Torn itch) The king's steward in Faery.

Zander – (Zan der) A chieftain of a tribe of people on the island.

Turn the page for a sneak peak of;
My Tormented Mage

MY TORMENTED MAGE

CHAPTER ONE - A WARM NIGHT

*T*he moon is full and high in the night sky. Even under the trees where they lie on the sand they can see it. It's early in the morning, still dark but the moon is bright. The September night warm near the city of Ageum. Kick and Drusey came to the secluded area of the waterfront to be alone. "It's marvelous here and I love it, what do you think, Drusey?" Kick asks.

"Yes, it's beautiful. Hey, will you rub my shoulders?" She appeals and pouts at her tall mage warrior. He's gorgeous and she can't help ogling him. His black curls are pushed back from his face giving her full view of his dark eyes. He gazes back at her marveling at her beauty. The allure of this place only emphasizes her looks.

Watching her he gets wrapped up in the view. He couldn't care less that she's miniature for a warrior gargoyle. She is only five feet three inches tall, a plus for him, he towers over her. Anyone, without a clue, might believe they could overpower his girl in a fight, having firsthand knowledge that's a mistake. He's seen her in a scrap. A rage flares in her when she fights, even during combat training. When she fights she battles to win.

Kick audibly gulps as Drusey turns her sexy gargoyle body toward him flirting. His heart skips a beat. Her tan skin has never experienced the light of day but is the color it would be if she spent hours soaking in the sun. Sandy blonde pieces of hair escape its braid and blows around her face as she pulls it in front of her. After rolling onto her side and turning toward him, she exposes her bare breasts. Instinctively he stares right at them, mouth open, eyes wide, and a stupid grin. Trying to behave, his focus travels up to the deep blue of her eyes. They're so deep they're almost purple and searching his own eyes.

"Come on, handsome, put your book down and rub my shoulders. We came to the shore to rest. I'm sore after our lessons in the arena. Please, will you put the textbook down and rub my back?" Her voice slides into a lower octave knowing the reaction it has on him.

Kick can't put down his spell book fast enough. Studying wasn't going well anyway he can't concentrate with her so close. He's sure she knows what she does to him and that he can't think straight seeing her topless.

"Of course, I'll rub your shoulders," Kick replies. *It gives me a reason to touch you.* With pleasure, he massages her back and wing arms using pressure techniques he studied in med school on her stiff muscles.

"Oh, that feels good," she moans. "What are you studying, anyway?"

Kick says, "Spells and more spells, that's all. Well, that's not all, we're learning new spells but also how to use them in the arena outside the castle. Did you know that castle Ilioilion is three hundred years old?" The castle is located within the walls of Ageum. The city while nearly four thousand years old is modern. They channel water throughout the city for sanitation and drinking. Although, it isn't the first city built in the area, it has been destroyed and rebuilt many times in its history. The last time was over three hundred years ago when another Greek city-state attacked and destroyed Ageum over a dispute involving the mother of Queen Iphigenia, Helen.

"No, I knew it was old, though. The castle is huge. Have you ever been inside?" Drusey asks.

"I've been in the castle on many occasions. When I was doing my medical education, I treated Queen Leta. That's how I started working there."

"Is it fancy inside the palace?" she asks excitedly.

"Yes, it is, not much has changed since I was first there either, except Iphigenia was the ruler then. It was before... well you understand." Kick stops, drops his head shaking it from side to side. The sadness in his eyes is obvious. Memories surface of the time in gargoyle history when Queen Iphigenia sacrificed her life to return the Ceorfan gargoyles to life. There were consequences, like turning to stone in the daylight. The Guild calls this process torpifying or torping. It's both blessing and curse––and the reason that the Ceorfan day begins when the sun goes down.

"Yes, I remember..." Drusey whispers.

He returns to the discussion about school, deflecting. "Did anyone ever tell you that the large arena is where we'll fight our acceptance battles into the Ceorfan Warrior Mage Guard?" That's the name of their school and will also be their job titles. If... they pass the rigorous schooling. Then they need to pass the virtually impossible tests plus receive the required number of referral documents. The Guild requires the Guard to be trustworthy and more than excellent soldiers. Graduation is nearing for Kick and Drusey, along with their classmates, they've gone to school for years. However, when they finish, their hardest training begins, improving their skills is a lifelong process on the job.

"Ouch, sorry, don't stop. I'm okay... just tweaked a nerve," Drusey cries.

"I'm sorry, I'll go easier. Did Peter hurt you in practice?" he asks. *I might need to talk to him about hurting my girl.*

Kick wasn't Drusey's partner in the arena tonight... again. Although the two of them don't know, the training masters figured out that he's in love with her and takes it easy on her. No way would she have learned half of what she did this evening if she had sparred with Kick. This evening she was matched with a smaller man, not weak by any stretch, named Peter. A larger gargoyle was Kick's partner his name is Kokkino Petra, or Kino as he's called. They had talked and found they have a lot in common. They're the largest of the cadet trainees. Both of their fathers are statesman working with the queen. They make perfect sparing partners. In their cases the Ceorfan statesmen have proven that they breed large sons.

Kick gently moves his lady's hair over, his big hands, covering the top of her small back and wings. He slides his hand down moving to other areas of her body. He skims down her sides, grazing the sides of her breasts, then down toward the small of her back and pushes at the band of her short skirt.

Before he starts something, he pleads, "Do you want to swim? Afterward we can get supper before you torp."

"Sounds fun! Last one in the water is a hydra!" she shouts jumping up running toward the water. As they reach the sea,

Kick takes her hand and drags her with him. The waves climb above them and they dive into the cool water. The fluorescent wave, lit by the full moon, speeds past them. They surface in a trough between ripples, both laughing and looking into each other as they plunge into the next swell. Because of her gargoyle nature she doesn't suffer the sting of the cold. But he's half human and half fae it's a shock to his system for a few minutes as his body adjusts. The sea is wonderful though, and it helps loosen their strained muscles, aching from practice earlier. They float for a while, fit as they are, they're not easily tired. He moves close to her and pulls her to him gathering her close for a kiss.

Soon, he is going to ask for her hand. His parents are happy about the match. The queen said she thinks he'll be a wonderful husband for Drusey. Kick has been friends with Queen Leta of the Ceorfan since she was a teenager and he was a young medical student. He helped her once when she was sick. He's a confidant to Her Majesty now. The laws of the Ceorfan Guild are clear on marriages; Kick must have the approval of his queen and the parents. He loves Drusey but he's a little anxious that she doesn't feel the same. Yet, when she has her strong body pressed against his, he thinks she just might. He decides right that second to brave it and move forward with his plan and ask her.

"Drusey, I have time off this evening. Will you go with me to the caves later? I'll bring us some breakfast, then we can go to class and on to training. What do you think?"

"That is a great idea. I would enjoy it. Now, let's get home so I can pose before sunrise. Come watch so you can get some of my energy," Drusey returns. When a gargoyle hardens it releases magic energy which radiates from their bodies during the torping process, the ones they love are welcome to absorb that energy. It's a family type sharing and is a widely practiced part of this culture. As excited as Kick is, this energy will also help him stay awake to lay the groundwork for his plans for tonight.

With hope in his fast beating heart, they race to her home where they greet her parents. His beautiful lady walks to her posing stage, a raised platform in the corner of the living area. She steps up, and her parents join her there. They all say together smiling, "Wings up, have a healing sleep."

A warm tingle covers Kick as he soaks up the magic that the family radiates when they torpify to stone in front of him. It gives him all the strength he needs for his plan. He says, "Goodbye, Drusey."

The Ceorfan gargoyles heal during torpification, no matter how badly they are hurt—it's a gift. The young man stares at her hardened stone body and hopes his lady sees him regarding her. He nods goodbye to her parents, recognizing they can see and hear him if they are still awake then twists around and leaves.

ACKNOWLEDGMENTS

Thank you, fans and readers my books. I appreciate each and every one of you. You are my prize. Please, if you enjoyed the books consider leaving me a review. It means more than you can imagine! But if you really hate them... please pass.

Thank you to my family, who is always supportive and helpful. My husband, I love that you are in my corner. I'm blessed to have you!

All my friends who are precious to me. Miki and Mine Guys and Goyles!

Christina and Brenda, you are the best PA's ever!

Thank you, Craig and Rob, and your wives Kathi and Peggy, you make everything possible. You are my best friends. I love you all. Thank you for your support! –– Miki Ward

OTHER BOOKS BY MIKI AND GARRETT WARD

Find us

FB Pages

Miki & Mine, Guys and Goyles Group
https://bit.ly/2CpH3BM

Miki's FB Author page
https://bit.ly/2yMlVSG

Garrett's FB Author page
https://bit.ly/2P3USwv

Bookbub
https://bit.ly/2J3FRFh

Amazon Author Page - Follow Miki
https://amzn.to/2Ey3qrk

Amazon Author Page - Follow Garrett
https://amzn.to/2yNYOr7